DEBORAH MALONE

DAHLONEGA
GOLD MUSEUM
Old Lumpkin
County Courthouse
1836

DEATH IN DAHLONEGA

A TRIXIE MONTGOMERY COZY MYSTERY

LAMP
POST

A LAMP POST BOOK

DEATH IN DAHLONEGA
  BY DEBORAH MALONE

ISBN 10: 1-60039-190-7
ISBN 13: 978-1-60039-190-3
ebook ISBN: 978-1-60039-714-1

www.lamppostpubs.com

DEATH IN DAHLONEGA

a Trixie Montgomery cozy mystery

Best Wishes

BY DEBORAH MALONE

Trust in the Lord with all your heart
and lean not on your own understanding.

Proverbs 3:5

ACKNOWLEDGEMENTS

I would like to thank the Lumpkin County Sheriff's Department, the Dahlonega Gold Museum, and the City of Rome Police Department for their help with police procedure.

I would like to thank Zack Waters for critiquing my manuscript and special thanks goes to Dawn Hampton who helped me breathe life into Trixie and Dee Dee.

Last, but certainly not least, I owe a debt of gratitude to Ashley Ludwig, Beverly Nault and Candice Prentice, my editors extraordinaire.

Dedication

"Death in Dahlonega" is dedicated to my family and friends
who supported me during my writing journey.

CHAPTER ONE

"Dahlonega, here we come!" I cheered, triumphant at the 10 miles to go sign. My knee ached from three hours in the car, my palms slick on the wheel from the harrowing twist of road.

"Here. Have some before I eat it all." My passenger, and oldest friend, Dee Dee, shoved a bag of trail mix under my nose.

I dug through and, finding only nuts, pushed it back. "You ate all the chocolate pieces!"

She muffled an unapologetic sounding apology, then continued singing along as Alan shifted to Clint Black.

My Jeep Cherokee bumped over a rut in the road as a semi sped downhill a trifle too fast. With a tight grip on the vibrating steering wheel, I rounded another curve on the mountain road.

I single-handedly gripped the wheel and cooled a sweaty palm on the air vent, thinking how this trip would propel my career from probationary to full-fledged reporter. This was my big chance to prove to my editor that I, Trixie Montgomery, could write an article with substance and flair, despite the rather routine subject matter. Who says you can't start a career after forty?

After all, "Gold Rush Days" in the North Georgia Mountains was hardly Pulitzer Prize material. Even the best had to start somewhere. Besides, what girl in her right mind could turn down an opportunity to take a little vacation while getting paid at the same time?

I reached over and squeezed my friend's hand. "Thanks for coming,

Dee Dee." I couldn't wait for a little antiquing, sightseeing, and plenty of good country cooking. What could possibly go wrong?

"Look!" Dee Dee pointed at something outside, misjudged, and slammed me hard in the nose. A spike of pain shot up through my eyes, to the top of my head.

"What?" I yelped, shooting a quick-glance to the rearview to see if it was bleeding. "You've broken my nose."

Dee Dee slid toward me until I thought she was going to sit in my lap. She leaned over, pointing out the window. "Over there. Those beautiful yellow trees."

"You almost broke my nose and scared the starch out of me to show me trees?"

"I'm sorry." She handed me a wad of tissues. "But have you ever seen anything so beautiful as these mountains in the fall?"

"Wade and I vacationed all over the United States, and the North Georgia Mountains are on the top of my favorites list." I longed to be in the passenger seat so I could study the view. But if you wanted to live while driving these roads you'd keep your eyes focused ahead, my ex-husband's voice reminded me with gritting annoyance.

"It's like God created a patchwork quilt with all the brightly colored leaves." Dee Dee rolled down the window a bit. "Mm. Fresh mountain air. Nothing smells as good, either." She stuck her head outside like a happy, oversized puppy.

"Careful there. I don't want to lose you."

She pulled her head back in. "I don't think there's any chance of me fitting through the window." She laughed at her own joke. "Where are we staying again?"

"I made reservations at the Dahlonega Inn," I said. "I got the last room, and only after I told the owner, Joyce, that I worked for *Georgia By the Way*. Turns out it's her favorite magazine."

Before we knew it, we arrived in Dahlonega. Hanging baskets full of geraniums hung from every light post. Second story porches adorned many of the clapboard structures. The shop-lined streets were filled with people milling about. A friendly driver waved us through the four-way stop.

The founding fathers had seen fit to arrange the buildings of Dahlonega in a square. The mountains served as a beautiful multi-colored backdrop. In the center stood the old Dahlonega Gold Museum, where most of my research would be carried out. I glanced at my camera, itching to get started.

We pulled into the Dahlonega Inn's gravel parking lot across from the town square. Brown-leafed Magnolias dotted the area.

Researching on-line, I'd learned the two-story clapboard house was originally built in 1895, and later turned into an inn in the early 1920's. I half expected a trio of flappers to saunter out the door.

"Come on Dee Dee. Let's head on in." I opened my door and struggled to reach the cane I kept behind my seat.

"Trixie, does your knee hurt? Hold on." Dee Dee reached behind the seat and shifted the cane where I could easily grab it, and I hobbled alongside her across the parking lot.

Anxious to get settled in, we entered the lobby of the Dahlonega Inn. The large room had been carefully decorated to resemble a homey replica of a Norman Rockwell parlor. A large stone fireplace adorned the wall across the room. Overhead, huge, hand-hewn beams supported a split cedar roof. Several comfy chairs perched in various corners of the room, and bright watercolor landscapes added a splash of color to the reception area. Visitors mingled while we maneuvered to the reception desk.

A smiling teenager stood behind the check-in counter, waiting to fill out the forms and hand us our keys. Dee Dee palmed them and was asking for the nearest facilities when the keys flew from her hand as a large man in an all-fired hurry plowed past, knocking her into me. Cane sailing from my hand, we smacked into the hardwood floor in a tangle of arms and legs.

"Get off me," I moaned.

Dee Dee, a woman who had not seen the petite section of the dress store for several years, struggled to get up. I tried to help, pushing at her without much success.

"Can't you see my friend uses a cane," she yelled at the retreating giant. "Why don't you watch where you're going you feather-brained lummox!"

He kept walking.

"You could at least apologize," Dee Dee shouted at his back. She helped me to my feet while several slacked-jawed onlookers stared. "Trix, are you all right? If I see him again...well I don't know what I might do."

A wide-eyed lady, with mouth agape, offered assistance. "Oh, I'm so sorry," she said. "Are either of you hurt? Can I help you?" She stuck out a shaking hand. "I'm Joyce, by the way. I'm the owner of this inn."

I realized she was the lady who had made our reservations. She was much older than her phone voice had led me to believe. A petite woman, she wore a bright red pantsuit. Her gray hair was cut in a stylish bob.

I took a quick physical assessment for any damage. "I think I'll survive. How about you Dee Dee?"

She huffed and did a hasty check. Though her body parts remained intact, I sensed her dignity had taken quite a hit.

"Well, I guess I'll live. That man was so rude. Maybe it was an accident, but he could have at least stopped to help." She adjusted her elastic waistband back into position and turned to Joyce. "Did you see him? He kept right on going." Dee Dee placed her hands on her ample hips.

I glanced at her bright orange pants and wondered how anyone could have missed her standing there. Her eyes still flashed with anger at the indignity that had been pressed upon us.

Joyce nodded. "Yes dear, I saw the whole thing. That's John Tatum. His family owns most of the property in Dahlonega. He eats at the inn quite often." Her words rushed out, then she paused, gazing after him. "He must have been upset about something, the way he kept going."

She retrieved my cane and handed it to me. Ever since my fall from Grace, a palomino with a short fuse, I'd been struggling with a bum knee. Despite therapy, there had been little improvement during the past four years.

The girl behind the desk summoned Joyce. She offered her apologies and left to handle the situation.

"Come on, Trixie." Dee Dee slung my purse on her shoulder while I steadied myself. "Let's go find some lunch."

"Sure, but don't you want to eat at the inn's buffet? I've heard it's to die for." Tasty smells filled the lobby. No wonder Mr. Tatum ate here often.

Dee Dee smoothed her clothes. "I need some fresh air."

We walked over to the town square. Dahlonega had done an excellent job of preserving its downtown and leaving its natural beauty unspoiled. The storefronts remained untouched by what some people would call progress. Old wood-front buildings displayed images of horses being tethered to a hitching post in front of the stores. In the distance, the Appalachian foothills faded away in a purple haze.

We found the cutest restaurant located on the second story, offering dining on an outside porch overlooking the town.

"After we finish eating, I need to head on over to the gold museum," I mentioned. "You know that ole' saying, 'work before fun.' Want to come with me?"

"Why don't you go ahead? I think I'll browse for a while. I don't plan on going home empty-handed. I promised Sarah I'd find some goodies for the store." Dee Dee owned an antique store, "Antiques Galore," in Vans Valley, and her octogenarian assistant, Sarah, would be thrilled.

I knew my friend; she'd keep her word. Eclectic boutiques, artisan stands, and even an old-fashioned candy shop lined the square, and they were calling her name. Cash registers rang as people bustled in and out of busy stores with full shopping bags. Before we parted ways, we agreed on a meeting place between four and five o'clock.

Dee Dee walked with me as far as the Dahlonega Gold Museum so she could carry my bag loaded with my laptop, camera and tape recorder. I ascended stairs to the grassy knoll where the museum stood like a sentinel watching over the town.

Inside the door, a middle-aged woman, dressed in crisp khaki pants and matching shirt, eyeballed visitors. She stood ramrod straight with her hands behind her back.

"Teresa Duncan," I said out loud as I read her name tag, and scrunched a smirk at the term "Ranger," lettered below her name.

"How may I help you?"

I explained I was researching an article for *Georgia By the Way*.

She displayed her first smile and told me Harv had called ahead, and that she'd be glad to help in any way she could.

Teresa spoke into a walkie-talkie, and within minutes a couple of young people appeared. They were dressed just like Teresa. "Trixie, let me introduce you to Tony Bowen and Rebecca Smith. They're rangers, too."

We shook hands, and I asked them a few questions.

"How about I take you on a tour?" Teresa asked.

"Do you mind if I take pictures while we talk?" I reached to get my all-important digital camera.

"Feel free to take as many as you want. This here's our mining exhibit. It explains three of the earliest methods of mining." She gestured in the direction of the room.

"Wow, look at all of these old tools on the wall." I snapped pictures of pickaxes, rock hammers, and old lanterns in rapid succession. As we walked through the building, I photographed dozens of dioramas, all devoted to gold mining.

"This was originally the courthouse for Lumpkin County," Teresa said. "It was built in 1836 and is the oldest courthouse in Georgia. It became a branch of the United States Mint in 1838. It remained so until 1861, after the Gold Rush." She pointed to a glass showcase housing original memorandums of gold bullion deposits and original deeds to property won in the land lottery.

I wrote as fast as I could. I also recorded our conversation so I wouldn't miss anything. Harv was a stickler when it came to details, and Teresa was a living, breathing, history book.

After the tour, Teresa excused herself to help other visitors while I walked outside and shot more photos of the building and surrounding area. The late afternoon sun arced as tourists mingled on the grassy lawn. A family of four posed for their picture under the Gold Rush Days sign, while a group of school children skipped toward a long yellow bus. These would make great shots to show the popularity of Gold Rush Days. One thing I'd learned about photography: a person usually had to take many shots to produce one good picture.

Back inside, Teresa offered to show me a film explaining the history of mining. Though I had researched a little online I didn't have enough material for my article. This would be a great opportunity to learn more about the mining process.

I checked my watch and saw it was closing in on a quarter 'til five. "My friend should be here any minute." I scanned the room to see if I could spot Dee Dee. "Could we wait for her?"

"Sure. We close at five o'clock, but I planned to stay late anyway, so y'all can watch the movie while I finish up my work."

"Thanks. I appreciate it." I placed my camera back in its case.

"If you need anything, ask Tony or Rebecca, and they'll help you," Teresa offered. After she escorted me to a bench where I could sit and wait, she left to find one of her assistants to run the projector.

I wiggled on the hard bench. We were upstairs where the film room was located. I hadn't seen this part of the museum yet, so I took advantage of the time. Getting up, I walked over and studied some of the old mining claims incased in glass. Outside onto the balcony, I could see the General Store across the way. I couldn't wait to explore the shops. But work came first, and I needed this article to shine.

I looked at my watch. It was five. *Where could Dee Dee be?* Shortly, I heard laughter floating up the staircase. Rebecca and Dee Dee entered the room.

"Trixie, you won't believe the deals out there!" Dee Dee held up both hands festooned with shopping bags.

"You feel like watching a mining movie?"

"Of course. Let's go!" Dee Dee said as if she'd been waiting for me instead of the other way around.

Rebecca directed us into a small auditorium behind a curtain on the other side of the display case. "I'll let Tony know you're ready for him to start the film." She gave us a brief salute and left the room.

Dee Dee stashed her bags on the empty seats beside her, and then we sat and waited quietly. A blast of music, accompanied by images of bedraggled, work-worn men and women, appeared on the screen.

The appearance of poverty-stricken workers dispelled the myth that all gold miners struck it rich. Large companies made most of the money. Backed by investors, these companies could provide the heavy equipment needed to find buried gold in the mountainous terrain. Many of the mountain people worked for these gold companies and never hit pay dirt themselves.

I was typing on my laptop when Dee Dee leaned over. "I've got to go tinkle. Where's the bathroom?"

"I saw one downstairs."

"OK, save my place." She nudged me with her elbow. "I'll be back in a few minutes."

I watched her scoot down the aisle past empty chairs. I had no doubt her place would be safe.

The majority of the movie passed with no sign of Dee Dee. Just as I was deciding to go see if she had fallen in, a blood-curdling scream jarred me from my thoughts, and triggered a thousand volts of electricity though my body.

I knew that scream! I maneuvered through the darkness, graceful as an elephant in a ballet, and hurried downstairs. Teresa, Rebecca, and Tony stood side-by-side blocking my line of sight. All three were on their cell phones. I squeezed in between them.

Dee Dee, pale as a ghost, gaped at me, eyes wide, squealing in horror. John Tatum, the man we'd literally run into in the Inn earlier, lay prostrate on the floor in a lake of coppery blood and scattered bills. And Dee Dee held a dripping pickaxe.

CHAPTER TWO

"Dee Dee, what happened? Are you all right?" I looked inside the mining room I had been in earlier.

I stepped forward and felt a tug. I turned around.

Teresa shook her head no. When she spoke, her voice sounded far away. "Ma'am you can't go in there."

"She needs me!" I said. Teresa didn't budge her hand from my elbow. A short time earlier, her authoritative character seemed like such an asset. Now it was just a pain in the asset.

"I've called 911. They're sending a deputy and an ambulance. They should arrive any minute. Why don't you go sit down? There are some chairs in the front area."

"I can't leave Dee Dee. But, I don't think I can stand up much longer." My lungs felt as heavy as that old safe in the lobby, and my legs wobbled like Jell-O.

Tony brought two chairs. I assumed one was for me and the other for Dee Dee. She wasn't going to need it. Dee Dee slid to the floor in a dead faint, dropping the axe.

As she hit the floor, two paramedics, dressed in blue uniforms and hauling red tackle boxes, rushed in.

One yelled, "I'll get the pass-out."

The other one replied, "I've got the trauma."

The minutes ticked by slower than the last drop of ketchup escaping from a bottle before Dee Dee opened her eyes and tried to sit up. The most inappropriate thought popped into my mind—*That's the quietest I've ever seen her.*

"Whoa there, take it easy." The young, blond paramedic gently steadied Dee Dee. Once she regained consciousness, he hurried over to where his partner worked on the lifeless body of John Tatum.

"Where is he?" barked a voice from behind. Two uniformed deputies barreled down the hallway.

"Jack, what've we got here?" The older of the two deputies addressed the paramedic.

"Well, sir, I suggest you call in the coroner. There are no vital signs."

The deputy walked over to where the paramedics attended the body and turned to his partner. "Secure the area, Ray, and don't let anyone in without my permission." He knelt down, and glanced at the lead ranger. "Teresa, don't leave them alone. I'll be there shortly to get everyone's statements."

I looked around to see who "everyone" was, and the only people I saw without the benefit of a uniform were me and Dee Dee.

Teresa helped Dee Dee up, and I took her other arm. "We'll go into my office. She can rest there until the sheriff gets through." She led us down the hall and into a sparsely furnished, wood paneled workspace. "Are you ladies okay?"

"Uh, yeah, we'll be fine." I didn't feel fine. And Dee Dee sure didn't look fine.

"Oh, no! Oh, no! Oh, no!" Dee Dee rocked back and forth in her chair as her vacant eyes stared straight ahead.

"Dee Dee, look at me! What's going on?" I placed my hands on her shoulders and leaned in towards her face. "What happened?"

A faint light of recognition appeared in her eyes. "Oh, Trixie, what are we going to do?" The rocking motion started again, and the light in her eyes dimmed.

"Dee Dee! Focus! And tell me what happened." My firm voice reverberated off the office walls. Her eyes filled with tears and spilled down her cheeks. I felt like a heel, and tried again. "It's all right. I'll stick by you no matter what happens." I reached over, grabbed a wad of Kleenex and handed them to her. I took deep breaths as I desperately tried to remain calm. My insides churned, and bile rose in my throat.

I was acutely aware that Teresa was in the room and could hear everything we said. I didn't care. Dee Dee might have been angry with him, and had called him a lummox and a brute, but murder him? Absolutely not.

"After I went to the bathroom I decided to check out the different rooms." Dee Dee's voice quavered. "I was going from room to room looking inside." Her chin quivered. "When I came to the mining room, I entered to get a closer look at the assortment of strange tools on the wall. I was half-way in the room when I saw that atrocious man lying in the corner with the pickaxe in his chest." She wiped a fresh stream of tears, then blew her drippy nose. "Oh, Trixie, it was horrible. What was I supposed to do? Let him lay there with an axe sticking out of him?"

I wanted to say, *Maybe call 911 and let them take it out*? But I bit my tongue instead, and shrugged.

"How did I know he was dead? I thought I was helping." She looked so sad. Her brown eyes under hooded eyelids reminded me of a Basset Hound. "Out of all the people who could have found that horrible man dead, why did I find him?" She foghorned into her tissue. "This doesn't look good does it, Trix?" Dee Dee voiced my thoughts.

"No, I'm afraid it doesn't."

The door squeaked, and our heads turned in unison as it opened, revealing the larger of the two deputies. His broad shoulders filled the doorway, and that dusting of gray hair gave him a distinguished look. I exhaled, long and slow, and for a moment forgot why we waited to speak with him.

"Ladies," he addressed us in a deep voice, rich with authority. "I'm Sheriff Jake Wheeler, and we have a murder on our hands."

CHAPTER THREE

D ee Dee and I looked at each other. She grabbed my hand and squeezed it in a death-grip. I managed a little squeeze in return.

"This is Deputy Sonny Ray." The sheriff gestured toward a man so skinny that, if he turned sideways, he'd be hard to find; that joke about Frank Sinatra disappearing behind his microphone flashed into my mind. But, this wasn't the time to think about jokes.

The handsome sheriff bore little resemblance to his deputy. Sonny Ray then smiled a ray of positive sunlight, sure to make someone confess to a crime they didn't commit. His mama hit it square on when she named him Sonny.

Sheriff Wheeler escorted Dee Dee from the office to unknown parts, leaving me with his sidekick. A chill ran through my body. I hugged myself for warmth. "Is she in trouble?" I fast scrubbed my arms. "How long 'til he brings her back?"

Deputy Ray rolled the office chair from behind the desk and took a seat.

"Whoa there Ms... Ms. Montgomery, right?"

"That's right, but you can call me Trixie."

"Trixie." He sunbeam smiled again. "I think I'm the one who's supposed to ask the questions."

That hundred-watt smile didn't fool me. I knew he was as serious as a riled up hornet's nest.

"I'll tell you what I can," he offered. "Sheriff Wheeler will bring your friend back as soon as he finishes questioning her." Deputy Ray adjusted his lanky frame and leaned back in the chair. He spaced out his words, long and deliberate. "Tell me what your business was at the museum and when you arrived." He held a poised pen over a notebook, ready to write.

"I'm here for a work assignment," I explained. "I work for *Georgia by the Way*, and I'm writing an article about Gold Rush Days."

"Go on." He wrote furiously in his notebook.

I wondered what he could be writing. I hadn't even said that much yet. Clearing my throat, I continued. "Teresa—Ranger Duncan, gave me a tour of the museum and then I went outside and took more pictures."

"Was Ms. Lamont with you during his time?" He stretched out his hand as if it had a cramp, his pen hovering above his pad.

"No, she was shopping. She came back around five." I checked my watch. I couldn't believe it was such a short time ago. "She came upstairs, and we were watching a movie on gold mining when she had to go to the ladies room. I told her there was one in the lobby."

His face turned a healthy shade of pink, "So, she left to use the ladies room..."

"Yes," I said. "She has to visit the bathroom more often than not." I prattled on, a fistful of nerves discussing her overactive bladder, until I noticed he'd stopped writing and stared at me.

I got back to the point, quick.

"While she was gone I heard this terrible scream. I knew right away it was Dee Dee. I thought something awful had happened to her." Pausing, I remembered we'd left my laptop and her shopping bags upstairs in the film room.

"What did you do when you heard her scream?" Deputy Ray leaned forward.

"I ran downstairs, of course." I didn't tell him I saw her standing there with the axe. I was sure he'd find out soon enough. A flashback of the scene popped into my head. I saw Dee Dee standing there with the lifeless body of John Tatum in the background, money strewn on the floor around him.

"Ma'am." He sat on the edge of his chair and looked me straight in the eye. "Is there something else you want to tell me?"

I shook my head.

"All right. I'll go find Sheriff Wheeler and let him know we're through here." He pulled out a business card. "If you think of anything else, please give us a call." He closed the door behind him, leaving me alone with my thoughts.

True to Deputy Ray's word, Sheriff Wheeler brought Dee Dee back a few minutes later. Dee Dee's haunted gaze found mine, her complexion looked like she'd stolen the white right off a lily. Shaking, she grabbed the doorframe with one hand, and reached for me with the other.

I stood up and headed straight for her. Nothing works better than a warm hug from a friend to let them know it's all right—even if it wasn't. "Oh, Trixie, Sheriff Wheeler wants me to stay around for the next couple of days."

"I'd like for both of y'all to stick around." He settled his hat on his head.

"Sheriff, you don't think Dee Dee had anything to do with this, do you?"

"Well, ma'am." He grabbed the doorknob. "She was found with the murder weapon. It's standard procedure in situations like this."

By the time we unloaded our luggage and returned to the inn, it was after nine. This was the first time we'd seen our room, and though it was nice and clean, the interior was time warped straight from the early 1900's. If the décor was meant to be realistic to that time period, then the decorators did their job well. The door led to the outside walkway, which wound around to the lobby. No wonder no one had reserved this room before I called. Even on this busy weekend.

The darkness outside matched the darkness I felt. Only this morning we had sung with Alan Jackson and eaten trail mix while we dreamed of a wonderful weekend. Our dream had turned into a nightmare.

"Trixie, what are we going to do?"

"I honestly don't know, Dee Dee. It feels like aliens have sucked my brains right out of my head. Are you mad at me for asking you to come?"

"No, not mad." Her pleading eyes begged for assurance. "Scared. Is the sheriff going to arrest me?"

"You wait and see." I faked optimism. "By morning, your involvement will be clarified. If that sheriff is half as good at solving crimes as he is good-looking, he'll have it figured out soon enough."

"You think so?" She spoke with an expectant tinge in her voice as she rubbed her palms together.

"It stands to reason, Dee Dee. You didn't even know John Tatum until today."

She managed a smile, but her watery eyes told another story. For her sake, I attempted to put on my big girl bloomers and show confidence—even if I didn't feel any.

"The truth is, Sheriff Wheeler asked me if I knew the victim. I told him Mr. Tatum knocked you down this morning." A sly grin crossed her face, and she voiced what I was thinking. "I didn't tell him about my little tirade, but he's bound to find out sooner or later."

"Let's hope he doesn't find out and blow it way out of proportion." I looked around for a dresser to hold my clothes.

We discussed the dilemma of calling our families. Should we, or shouldn't we? We decided to wait until tomorrow. No reason to worry them needlessly.

A loud growl erupted from my stomach, accompanied by a burning, gnawing pain. A blatant reminder of when we'd last eaten.

"My lands, Trixie. It's a good thing we're not in public."

"No worse than the noises you make all night," I shot back. "I'll scout the lobby for food. I need to eat so I can take some pain medicine." I rubbed my knee. The relentless ache alerted me of the impending knee replacement in my near future. As a teenager and young woman I actively played sports. I didn't realize the beating my knees took until adulthood. I compounded the damage when I fell from that danged horse.

"What can you find to eat this time of night?"

"I remember seeing a refreshment area with coke and cracker

machines. Not the Waldorf, but better than nothing. I'll get you a bite, too."

"I don't feel like eating," she replied.

Uh oh, not a good sign. I could count on one hand the number of times when Dee Dee lost her appetite.

Timing is of no consequence to memories. Maybe food was the trigger. Vivid images flashed through my mind, replaying the time when one of Dee Dee's precious cats choked on a chicken wing. Like any good mother, she reacted immediately. Then panic set in and she started slinging the cat around in circles, yelling "I killed him! I killed him!"

Gary, Dee Dee's late husband, rescued the cat and discovered a jagged bone stuck in the roof of Ziggy's mouth. After Gary fished out the bone, the dazed cat recovered nicely. Too bad Dee Dee didn't fare as well—it took her several days to get over the shock.

CHAPTER FOUR

I grabbed my cane. It wasn't that far to the lobby, but my knee felt as supportive as a worn out bra. The lighting outside was barely enough to illuminate the pathway. Shadows danced around me.

I reached the lobby to find it deserted; not unusual at this time of night. The quietness of the room heightened my nerves.

The snack room proved easy enough to find, much easier than finding my change. As I fumbled around in my bag, the hair on the back of my neck suddenly stood at attention.

I turned, quickly, and spied a lanky man staring my way, blocking my exit. I dropped my bag, and contents spilled in all directions.

"Please. Let me help you." The stranger scrambled to pick up my belongings.

Embarrassment shrouded me like a cloak as a tampon rolled across the floor.

"I'm sorry. I didn't mean to startle you. I'm Leroy Roberts. I help Aunt Joyce run this place." He seemed apologetic, but I couldn't shake the feeling he'd been watching me.

"Shoot. You took ten years off of my life."

"I'm so sorry." He smiled sheepishly as he handed me my stuff. His eyes wandered to my cane. "Can I help you with anything?"

"I was trying to find change. I wasn't having much luck."

"Come on in the office with me." He pointed to a door not far from where we stood. "I'll be glad to help you get what you need."

I warily followed him to the office where he opened a cash drawer and traded me for a stack of ones. Like a shadow, he accompanied me back to the snack room. I bought a bountiful supply of drinks and food, enough to last us through the night. He kindly offered to carry my stash of crackers and cookies back to the room.

"Uh, no thank you." I thanked him for his help, and bade him good-night. I couldn't get back to my room fast enough, so I hurried as quickly as I could hobble.

"Where've you been, Trixie? I started to look for you." Sprawled out on the bed, atop a beautiful white Chenille bedspread, Dee Dee didn't look like she'd planned on going anywhere.

"You won't believe what happened!" I explained how Joyce's nephew appeared out of nowhere and scared the starch out of me.

"He stood close enough to see my gray hairs—that is if I had any." I ignored the snort Dee Dee rendered and continued. "I don't know. He seemed nice enough, but I had this sense he'd been watching me."

"I'm sorry Trixie." Dee Dee picked at invisible lint on the cover. "I guess we're both on edge after today's events. Who wouldn't be? But, what if it was a coincidence you turned around the same time he was going to speak."

"I suppose you're right. I was on my last nerve and jumpy as a cat in a room full of dogs."

"What did you get to eat?" She licked her lips, and browsed my purchases with keen eyes. "I think I might be able to handle a little something."

I rummaged through the goodies. "I've got cheese crackers, trail mix, and some pretzels. What do you want?"

She sat up on the bed. "I'll take the pretzels and some cheese crackers if you have enough. Did you get me a diet drink?"

As she reached for and slurped my soda, I breathed in relief. Nice to catch a glimpse of the old Dee Dee.

Except for munching sounds, quietness enveloped the room as we sat on our respective beds. We made up for the dinner we didn't feel like eating.

I relinquished dibs on the bathroom to Dee Dee. Thirty minutes later, she stepped out, looking like the cat's meow—literally. Dee Dee wore bright red pajamas covered with white cats. Those red pj's on Dee Dee conjured up images of Mrs. Claus.

Worried and completely worn out by the day's adventures, I stumbled to the bathroom. The décor reminded me of my grandmother's house, more utilitarian than glamorous. An antique chain dangled from the one lone bulb on the ceiling. A muslin cloth curtain hid the exposed pipes under the sink. In the corner of the room stood a claw foot tub, deep enough to get lost in, and I couldn't wait to sink into a tub full of hot water and soak sore muscles wound tighter than an old pocket watch.

Relaxed and ready for bed, I exited the small sanctuary. The cacophony of rattling sounds coming from Dee Dee alerted me she was either asleep or choking on something. Spying her a long moment, I decided she was asleep. I lay in my unfamiliar bed rehashing the events of the day. I wondered how in the world we got into this mess; worse yet, how in the world would we get out of it?

Only a little while ago, the room seemed quaint and alive with history. Lying in the darkness, it seemed oppressive and full of unsettled ghosts. I tossed and turned as sleep eluded me, and stared into the black night for what seemed an eternity. My mind drifted into a dreamlike state.

I stood in the town square. An angry mob was making its way to the courthouse. My heart rate accelerated as I realized they were headed for Dee Dee, who stood holding a pickaxe in her bloodied hands.

The mob drew closer and closer, familiar as well as unfamiliar faces appeared. Sheriff Wheeler, Deputy Ray, Joyce, and her nephew, Leroy Roberts, stood out from the others. Contorted faces and furious, bulging eyes indicated they had not come to help.

What was worse, a lifeless, pale, zombie form of John Tatum, with a gaping hole in his chest, led the pack. A devious grin covered his face.

Death was closing in!

CHAPTER FIVE

Seconds before death's hand closed around my throat, I shot straight up, a scream on my lips. Darkness shrouded the eerily still room. Fear had drenched my night clothes in sweat as if I'd completed a mini-marathon.

After a few breaths, the cobwebs cleared my mind. I strained to get my bearings in the unfamiliar surroundings, clutched the covers tight under my chin, and sent up a prayer. *Please Lord, keep us from harm. May my sleep be free from nightmares.*

I fluffed up my pillows and lay down. Dee Dee's familiar snores wafted from the next bed, and lulled me to sleep.

Morning came way too soon.

Dee Dee sat on her bed, legs crossed. "Trixie, please tell me I dreamed I found a dead man." Her gaze pleaded for me to agree.

"More like a nightmare. Let's hope the sheriff has found the person responsible." Images of the handsome Jake Wheeler flashed in my head. I smiled. After had Wade left me, I had thought I would never be able to admire another man. Moisture filled my eyes, and I blinked hard and changed the subject. "Are you hungry?"

Dee Dee's eyes lit up like a night star. "Is a black bear black?" She giggled at her own joke, and patted at her midsection. "Let's go see what they have in the dining room. Those crackers are long gone."

Both dressed in slacks, short sleeve shirts, and comfortable shoes, Dee Dee and I prepared to meet the challenges of the day. The colorful combination of Dee Dee's ensemble, next to my own blend-in-with-the-crowd khakis, put a smile on my face. The beaded, multi-colored necklace and the copious bangles on her wrists completed the fashion in true Dee Dee style.

Outside, the cool mountain air was a balm to my spirit. The sweet smell of gardenia pleased my nose. "The sun is trying for all its worth to peep out. I predict a beautiful day." I gave her a poke, longing to cheer Dee Dee up. But it was going to take more than a perfect fall day to work that wonder.

In the cozy lobby a few people stood scattered around, some looked at brochures, while others relaxed on overstuffed sofas. Arrows pointed down the hall and to the right, and the smell of bacon lured. Crammed with tables, the area looked more like a breakfast nook than an actual dining room. People crowded around the breakfast buffet like pigs at feeding time. We lined up for our turn at the trough, me committed to sticking with whole grains and yogurt.

With Dee Dee blocking like a Bulldogs linebacker, we hurried to beat a little old couple to the only empty table by the window viewing the town square. At the last minute we acquiesced. It wasn't long before another table by the window became available.

Outside, merchants and artisans lined both sides of the streets. Participants set up their various booths, getting ready for the enormous crowd guaranteed that weekend. Soon, you'd be lucky to see daylight between the excited tourists.

"Wow, I guess Gold Rush Days brings in the crowds." Dee Dee buttered a homemade biscuit. Golden yellow liquid slid off the sides of the hot treat. I stared at my granola and yogurt. Now my mouth watered.

Dee Dee must have misunderstood my expression. "I know. I know. We planned on a fun weekend. I'm sorry."

I leaned in closer to Dee Dee, my attention focused on the biscuit. "You can quit apologizing Dee; it's not your fault someone killed Mr. Tatum." Temptation overpowered me. I sneaked half a biscuit from her plate, and jammed it into my mouth. "Sorry." I spoke through the crumbs.

Dee Dee moved the other half out of my reach. "I'm always getting into some sort of trouble. Losing my temper. Causing a scene."

"Not your fault," I muffled through a mouthful. "If the attitude he portrayed yesterday is normal behavior, then I suspect a few people wanted to murder him." I surveyed my plate, then hers. My granola and yogurt looked unappetizing next to Dee Dee's plate of sausage, biscuits, gravy, hash browns, and scrambled eggs.

"Back in a second," I murmured and headed back to the breakfast buffet. While there, I overheard a couple of women talking about the murder.

I grabbed two biscuits, put them on my plate, and lingered by the packets of jelly and jam to eavesdrop.

The taller of the two women spoke, heaping a steaming scoop of scrambled eggs to her plate. "It was probably the wife. Well his ex-wife."

Her companion chimed in with a wag of the grits spoon, and went on about how his ex-wife, Tammy, should really be on the suspect list.

I screwed my lip and selected a handful of strawberry jams. Interesting how she didn't hold back when it came to telling people how she felt about him. And it wasn't complimentary either. They moved forward toward the drink dispensers.

Someone gave me a gentle nudge from behind. My cue to move on down the line. I eyed my plate on the way back to the table. My new choices, hash browns, sausage, and buttered biscuits, supplied enough grease for a lube job on a small car. *Oh well; what's a girl to do on vacation?* Besides, yesterday's stress probably added up to some calorie use. At least it made me feel better to think so.

We were quiet as we crammed food into our mouths, much like everyone else in the room. I looked up between bites and spotted Joyce across the crowded room. Her eyes widened. She threw up her hand in greeting and veered our way.

"Here comes Joyce," I stage whispered.

Dee Dee looked up and scowled. "Well, she can walk on by for all I care. I'm not in the mood to talk." She stuffed another bite of egg into her mouth, guaranteeing she wouldn't be able to say a word.

"Grouchy," I whispered as Joyce approached, but I knew how Dee Dee felt. I wanted to eat in peace, and I especially didn't want to be reminded of the previous night.

"Hi! How are y'all doing this morning?" Without waiting for an invitation, Joyce plunked down in an empty chair and made herself at home. Dee Dee's eyes glittered with irritation. "I guess after yesterday's happening, y'all aren't doing too good."

Dee Dee and I exchanged a glance. Her expressive eyes spoke volumes. *Brilliant deduction, Sherlock.* I fake-wiped my mouth to stifle a giggle.

"You might say that. But breakfast is helping. The food is great. I don't want it to get cold." I shoveled some hash browns in my mouth, hoping Joyce would get the message, but she didn't. Instead she planted her elbows on the table, oblivious to our emotions.

Dee Dee heaved a sigh and ate more sausage. Joyce glanced around the room then leaned in toward us. "I thought I should warn you."

Dee Dee stopped chewing. "Warn us?" she asked through a mouth full.

"About what?" I flicked a glance to the ladies I'd overheard in line, and saw them staring. Were people already talking about us?

Joyce took a deep breath. "Sheriff Wheeler came by this morning, and we had a long talk. He asked me what took place between Dee Dee and John Tatum. I told him what I knew. I didn't want to get you girls in trouble, but I felt obligated to tell the truth. The truth is always the right thing to say, don't you think?"

Joyce squirmed in her chair.

I took a quick gander at her. Petite and downright skinny. Wrinkles lined her face, but they faded next to her beautiful smile. She exuded friendliness that bordered on annoying. That friendliness just might allow us an intimate look inside the community.

Dee Dee's plump hand reached over and patted Joyce's skinny one. I recognized the wide-eyed, insincere look on her face. I knew a false endearment was coming. "Sure, Sugar, you did the right thing."

"It's terrible." Joyce's gray bob swung as she shook her head. "I still can't believe John Tatum is dead. He was such a leader in the community." Someone from the front of the room called for her. She scooted her chair back and excused herself. "Be right back, girls."

Dee Dee folded her napkin and laid it on top of her empty plate. "I've lost my appetite."

"I have, too." I put my fork down, noticing the way the grease from the sausage was congealing on my plate.

"So much for your theory, Trix. I'd wager the sheriff is looking at me as a suspect." An un-lady like burp erupted from her mouth. "Excuse me." She blotted the soiled napkin to her mouth.

"And you said I made unpleasant noises?" I crossed my arms and leaned back to stare at her.

"Well, I'm entitled. I could be jailed for the rest of my life."

"Oh, come on," I said with as much conviction as I could muster. "That sheriff looks like a smart man. Surely he can figure out you're no murderer."

Dee Dee snorted. "Looking smart doesn't count for anything. Time will tell." A slight smile came to her lips. "He *is* good looking. If not for the circumstances, I wouldn't mind him looking at me."

I forced a laugh along with her. My breakfast churned in my stomach, and Dee Dee eye's were dark with concern. Good looking or not, the sheriff and his new information made me nervous. Perhaps we should keep our ears open and learn a little more about John Tatum, just to help the sheriff along.

CHAPTER SIX

Before I could tell Dee Dee my plan, Joyce hurried back to our table and sat down. I heard Dee Dee groan, and I kicked her under the table, sure that Joyce had heard her. Now that I had gone into information collecting mode, I didn't want to discourage the innkeeper, but once again she was oblivious to anything but herself and began to talk as though she'd never stopped.

"As I was saying, he did a lot of things to help the community. Not everyone liked him, but Mr. Tatum always pitched in if the need arose." Joyce waved to an older couple across the room and hollered out a hardy 'hello.' "He could be overpowering when he exerted his authority and that rankled some feathers."

My ears perked up like a coon dog on a scent. "Are you saying he made enemies around town?"

"I guess you could say that. He was known for using strong-armed tactics to get what he wanted." Joyce started stacking plates and swiped up several empty jam and sugar packets. "As you experienced first-hand, he had the personality of Attila the Hun. I suppose you could say he had a heart of gold and a fist of steel. Nonetheless, I felt sorry for him. He was going through some hard times." Her tone didn't match her words. I wondered if she really felt sympathy for him.

Dee Dee and I looked at each other, her brows rose and fell. I felt pretty sure we thought the same thing. It was possible that several of the town's folk wanted John Tatum dead.

"What bad things?" I watched Joyce clatter a cup full of silverware and restack the plates, and tried again. "What had he been going through?"

"His father, John senior, died about six months ago." She kept moving the plates from one place to another. "He was patriarch of the family business. After his death, everything was left to John—including all the problems his father left behind.

"And it's common knowledge he's recently gone through a nasty divorce." Joyce lifted, dropped her shoulders with a sigh. "His ex-wife, Miranda, made sure everyone knew. Anyway, Miranda found out he'd been messing around with his secretary. He was gone from their house faster than he could say, 'I'm sorry.'

"You go girl!" I shoved a fist in the air for emphasis.

Joyce looked at me, eyes wide with surprise. Dee Dee, however, just shot a knowing look to my pain. I didn't realize I'd spoken aloud my thoughts. Heat warmed my cheeks. "Uh, I didn't mean to say that out loud."

"Honey, you just voiced what I was thinking." Dee Dee squeezed my arm.

Dee Dee, no stranger to loss, stood by my side as staunch supporter and friend this past year during my own divorce. When her husband, Gary, died suddenly after an undiagnosed heart problem several years ago, Dee Dee's enduring faith through the tough times, as well as the good, set an example for me to follow.

To lighten the mood, Dee Dee asked Joyce, "What happened after she turned the two-timing, low-down, scum-sucking, no-good son of a snake out of the house?"

I choked on a mouthful of lukewarm coffee. Joyce's startled gaze darted between me and Dee Dee. I laughed out loud. "Well, Dee Dee, why don't you tell us how you really feel."

"I just did."

Joyce finally laughed and patted Dee Dee's arm. "Miranda went for where it hurt the most—the wallet. I heard it got nasty in court. Miranda's attorney exposed all of John's indiscretions. A woman judge sat on the bench that day, and she made John pay through the nose." Joyce shook her head as she spoke, her bob bouncing back and forth.

"How did you learn about the court proceedings?" Dee Dee asked.

"We're a small town. Everybody knows somebody who knows somebody, and news travels faster than butter on a hot biscuit." Joyce wiped the crumbs off the table and smoothed the tablecloth. "Miranda is president of the Historical Society. I was at the meeting where she spent the majority of the time enlightening the members of John's affair. She was mad as a wet setting hen!" Joyce had a faraway look and her shoulders shuddered.

I couldn't blame Miranda. Being betrayed by the one person in life you trusted, beyond a shadow of a doubt, was devastating.

Joyce voiced my sentiments. "Yeah, but you can't blame her. I'd be mad, too." She stood and gathered the stacked dishes, cups, and utensils. "Time to go see about my customers; got to keep them happy. Let me know if you need anything."

"Joyce!" I Columbo'ed her and smiled as she turned around. "One more thing. Where can we get in touch with Miranda? I might want to interview her for my magazine article since she's in the Historical Society."

"She owns an antique shop on the square, The Antique Boutique. She works most of the day. She'll probably be busy today though, it being Gold Rush Days and all." And with that, she hurried off to take care of business.

Dee Dee shot a shark-toothed grin. "Are you really going to interview Miranda for your article, Trixie?"

"Sure, why not? And while I'm interviewing her I might happen to ask her a few questions about her ex-husband. I'd say she had a motive for murder. Since I've found out about Wayne, there's been more than one occasion I dreamed of doing bodily harm to that two-timing cheater."

My poor heart ached talking about it. I quickly prayed for forgiveness for such angry thoughts. I'd begun to recover, but was still in the healing process. Band-aids of hurried prayers and half-hearted pep-talks held my fragile heart together.

What if John's ex-wife had taken her red-hot anger and humiliation to the extreme and acted out those feelings? It was possible.

Dee Dee's expression softened. She put her arm around my waist. "Trix, you know it's all right to have thoughts and feelings that aren't in our best interest. It's what we choose to do with those emotions that can get us in trouble. Why, I don't know how many times I've said, 'If Gary hadn't died, I'd have killed him for making me a widow.'" She gave me a squeeze as I wiped a tear from my cheek.

I'd just blown my nose when Sheriff Wheeler sauntered up with his sidekick, Deputy Ray. I stashed the Kleenex in my pants pocket.

"Good morning, ladies." The sheriff touched the tip of his hat, like any good southern gentleman's mama taught him to do. "I hope you slept well last night."

His Cheshire-cat grin stepped on my last nerve. "Well, of course we didn't sleep well, Sheriff. My friend *did* find a dead body yesterday." *Like, I needed to remind him.*

He shot me a wickedly handsome smile. "You're right, Ms. Montgomery—may I call you Trixie?" I nodded, and he continued. "Both of you experienced a traumatic affair. Maybe this job has left me a little too jaded. Please accept my apologies."

I nodded at his honey covered words, and felt the hard shell of my resistance begin to melt.

"We do accept your apologies, Sheriff." Dee Dee pushed me aside. "And you can call me, Dee Dee." She giggled like a schoolgirl and offered her hand. As they shook, the bangles on her wrist played a jaunty, ching-ing melody. "I reckon that means we can call you Jake."

He didn't answer. *I guess not.*

Sheriff Wheeler turned and gestured towards a man dressed in a Sunday go-to-meeting suit. "Let me introduce Agent Jeff Cornwall from the Georgia Bureau of Investigations. Any time there's a crime on state property, the GBI is called in to perform an investigation."

Agent Cornwall, light pole thin, loomed over Sheriff Wheeler. I had a mental picture of the agent as Abe Lincoln on stilts and almost burst out laughing. I quickly covered my mouth to hide my mirth. I could tell my nerves were frayed like an old electric wire.

"We've questioned several witnesses present in the lobby yesterday when Dee Dee had the unfortunate confrontation with John Tatum. There might be more to it than she suggested." The sheriff looked directly into Dee Dee's eyes. "We'd like for you to come down to the station so we can question you further."

Dee Dee's nostrils flared. "If I'd'a known you intended to arrest me, I sure wouldn't have accepted your apology much less shake your hand." Her flirtatious smile gone, she shot him a scathing look.

"I'm not going to arrest you. I just want to ask you a few more questions. This shouldn't take long," Sheriff Wheeler said. "We're going back to the office, why don't you ride with us." Then, turning those baby blues towards me, he asked, "Why don't you come by in an hour or so? We should be through by then."

I offered him the sweetest smile. "Of course I will." I addressed Dee Dee. "Just call me on my cell when you're done, and I'll come in a jiffy." I avoided eye contact with the sheriff. I gave Dee Dee a quick hug and hoped she didn't see the tears pooling in my eyes.

"All right," he addressed the two men standing beside him. "Let's get on our way."

Agent Cornwall, Deputy Ray, Sherriff Wheeler, and a forlorn looking Dee Dee traipsed out of the dining room with tourists looking on. I couldn't shake the notion that Dee Dee looked like a lamb being led to slaughter.

CHAPTER SEVEN

I returned to the stifling air of our tiny room. The walls seemed to close in on me. My mind tripped to the time I wandered away from my parents in Redford's Five and Dime. I had never been so glad to see my Mama when she found me. Feeling like that same lost child, I pulled my cell phone from my purse and dialed her up.

"Mama, I'm so glad you're at home." Mama's an angel on earth. She possessed the patience of Job, the strength of Samson, and the faith of Abraham. She had to, being the sole caregiver for Nana, her strong-willed, quirky aunt.

"Trixie, what is it? Are you okay?" Mama must have heard the strain in my voice.

"Yes and no. We've run into a little trouble." I wondered how much I should tell her. "There was a murder yesterday at the Gold Museum." At Mama's sharp intake of breath, I continued. "We were watching a film on gold mining when Dee Dee went to the bathroom. She found the body." My bottom lip quivered.

Mama gasped. "Oh my goodness, how horrible! How's she doing?"

"She's doing fine, Mama." I didn't want her to worry any more than necessary. "They took her to the sheriff's department to ask her a few questions. I think it's only a formality." *Please forgive me for stretching the truth.* I prayed it was true as a sick thread of worry for Dee Dee wove through my stomach.

"Do you need me to do anything?" Mama asked.

In my mind's eye, I could see the worry etched on her face.

"No Mama, but I'll let you know if I do. How are things at home? Is Nana behaving?" I asked, knowing good and well she was probably giving Mama a hard time, her quirky behavior a cover up for getting away with her antics. I'd seen some of Nana's mischief first hand when Mama had offered me a place to stay after the divorce. Wade had made so many bad investments we lost everything, including our house.

A hearty laugh came through the phone. "If you call Nana inviting Beau to come over for dinner behaving—then yes, she's behaving."

"What? She's been trying to marry me off to him since the third grade." I had to laugh, too, thinking of the countless times she'd tried to set us up. I've told her up and down I was done with men, but she never listened.

Mama and I had learned it was easier to laugh at Nana's meddling. We'd discovered too many times the alternative was to cry.

"Thanks, Mama, I appreciate it. I've got to go, but I'll call you back later."

"Please keep me updated, and don't worry. Nana and I will take care of Bouncer. She loves your dog." Images of Nana in her nightgown, coming to my rescue, popped in my mind. A forewarning?

"By the way, Jill called, and she's doing fine. She's looking forward to winter break." Jill, my daughter, was and a junior at the University of Georgia.

"Mama, if she calls again please don't mention the murder. It'll just upset her."

We talked a few more minutes and said our good-byes. "Sweetheart, please be careful. We love you," she said, her voice full of concern.

"Okay, Mama, I'll be careful. I love you and Nana, too." I disconnected the call.

I rummaged around and found a tablet and pen. I needed to make a list of questions to be answered in order to help Dee Dee. I needed a place to start.

1. Who had a reason to kill John Tatum?

2. Why would they want him dead?

3. How did they know where he was going to be?

After I made my list, I wandered to the bathroom to clean my face. The pasty reflection in the mirror shocked me. I'd arrived feeling like a forty-something diva, and now looked like a tired, red-eyed woman. I reapplied my make-up for damage control and left to pick up Dee Dee.

CHAPTER EIGHT

The morning sun illuminated the red, yellow, and orange leaves. I looked up through the colorful foliage to see a robin egg blue sky, and smiled at the high definition day for the merchants as well as the tourists.

I decided to drive to the sheriff's department. I didn't trust my knee to hold up for the long trek. When my car started on the first turn of the ignition, I heaved a huge sigh of relief. It had been hit or miss lately.

The town square was closed to traffic. Following the directions I'd been given, I drove the back roads. The red brick building was newer than its neighbors, but a talented architect had designed it to blend in with the older historic buildings.

I entered the front door into a sparsely furnished lobby. A uniformed young woman, who manned the front desk, was so intent on something she didn't notice me until I cleared my throat. She looked up with wide eyes and slid a gossip magazine underneath a folder. "May I help you?"

"Yes, I'm Trixie Montgomery, and I'm here to pick up my friend Dee Dee Lamont." I looked around the lobby. No Dee Dee.

"Oh, yes, Ms. Montgomery. The sheriff told me when you came by to inform you that the interview is taking a little longer than expected. He asked if you could come back in an hour or so. They should be finished by then." The blonde young woman, smacking a wad of gum, looked like she should be sitting behind a desk in high school.

What choice did I have? "Sure, I'll be back to pick her up." I turned and left her to finish reading about Justin Bieber.

Outside, tourists roamed the busy streets. An older couple, decked out in matching coral shirts, wore worn faces and kind smiles. A young mother held the hand of a rambunctious toddler as she maneuvered a baby stroller over the curbs and through the maze of excited people. Children of all ages lined up at the candy apple booth. They were carefree and oblivious to the trouble Dee Dee and I faced.

Why did the sheriff have his suspicions focused on Dee Dee? According to Joyce, more than one person had a stronger motive to kill Tatum. I knew I had made the right decision to help my friend. She would do no less for me.

My sore knee throbbed. I strolled to the car to retrieve my trusty cane. While there, I decided to face the inevitable and call Harv, my editor. A sweet voice answered the phone. "Good morning, *Georgia By the Way*. This is Belinda. May I help you?"

Lord, please don't let him be in the office. I had no idea how Harv would react to our circumstances. I didn't want to know.

"Hi Belinda. This is Trixie." I fiddled with a string hanging from my shirtsleeve.

"Oh, hi, Trixie. You still in Dahlonega? Do you want to speak to Harv?"

Obviously, my prayer hadn't reached its destination in time.

"Uh, what kind of mood is he in?" Harv had a heart of gold, but could be quick tempered.

"Well, he's a little jumpy this morning. But I'm sure he's feeling much better since he's had his black coffee and jelly doughnuts. Do you want me to put you through?"

"Sure, thanks." I watched the flow of tourists as I waited on Harv.

"I thought you'd never call," Harv's voice blasted across the line. "What's going on? Are you making progress on the article?" I could imagine Harv sitting at his desk, phone in one hand and a Tootsie Pop in the other. He'd made the switch from cigars after the scare with his heart.

"Uh, yes and no, Harv," I said with trepidation in my belly.

"What kind of answer is that?" Harv barked. "Have you or haven't you?"

"We've run into a little snag." I gave a nervous pull on the hanging thread, and the hem of my sleeve raveled.

"Spit it out. I don't have all day to yap on the phone. What kind of snag?" I could hear him crunch down. Probably cherry red, his favorite.

While he chewed, I brought Harv up to speed, from the lobby exchange, to the gold museum movie and Dee Dee's bathroom wandering, finishing with her standing over the bloody corpse.

This was my last assignment before my six-month probation period was over. John Tatum's murder case could result in the demise of my job. Harv could kick me out on my keister faster than a racehorse springing from a starting gate.

The silence on the other end of the phone was deafening.

CHAPTER NINE

A roaring boom broke the silence and I jerked the phone from my ear. "Montgomery! What have you gotten yourself into?"

I breathed a sigh of relief. Instead of being angry, he actually sounded happy. And then, in his usual fashion, he turned disaster into, "a story that could net us the Georgia Magazine of the Year Award."

I got out pencil and paper to take notes while Harv barked new orders. "Trixie, you need to research murders that occurred during the original gold rush days. And find out what you can about this Tatum character. We'll run this as a feature. 'Gold Rush Days Turn Deadly,'" he tried out a headline, a fresh tootsie paper crackling in the background. "Maybe we could devote the entire issue to Dahlonega if you can pull this off."

This definitely meant more work. I had my hands full now with the articles and helping Dee Dee. My heart pounded at the assignment. "I'll do what I can." My voice squeaked. "I mean, I'll get the facts, boss!"

The line went dead. He'd hung up on me, leaving me with the task of dredging up old murders.

I exited the car, shoved my cell phone into my pant's pocket, and grasped my cane tight. It fit secure in my palm, like holding on to an old friend.

The streets boasted an assortment of people coming and going. The blending of colorful clothes reminded me of a patchwork quilt. The clippity-clop of horse's hooves prompted me to turn in time to see a horse drawn carriage coming down the street. Smiles and squeals of excitement escaped from young children in the carriage.

I stopped a woman towing a child busy with an ice cream cone, and asked her where The Antique Boutique was located. I was more than embarrassed when she said, "Right behind you, sweetie." She offered me a smile and bent down to wipe her toddler's chocolate-covered face.

A bell jangled my arrival into the musty shop. Once inside, country charm surrounded me. Reconditioned antique furniture was jammed into every nook and cranny. Handmade wood furniture, from bedposts to birdhouses, filled the right corner of the shop. An attached sign revealed a local man had carved the unique pieces.

"Hi. May I help you?" I turned to see a beautiful woman smiling at me. Her skin reminded me of evaporated milk—creamy but not white. I'd be willing to wager the family farm she'd never been plagued by teenage acne! Dark blonde hair and a figure to kill for completed the look.

"Um, yes. I'm looking for Miranda Tatum," I stammered.

"That's me. Are you looking for something special?" She took a rag tucked in her belt and polished the top of a table.

"I love this homemade furniture," I gushed, running a hand over the smoothed arm of a rocking chair.

"It's become one of our best sellers. People are fascinated with anything homemade. They can't get enough of it. This is a great weekend for sales."

I thought I could see dollar signs in her big green eyes.

"I believe you're right, but I didn't come to buy anything. I want to know if I can interview you. Joyce Johnston at the Dahlonega Inn told me you're president of the Historical Society."

I looked at the table she'd been polishing and was surprised to see my reflection.

"Yes, I am," she said. "But this isn't a good time. As you can see, it's already hectic." She smiled politely, but turned to walk away.

"It won't take long, I promise. I'm writing a story on Gold Rush Days and want to feature The Antique Boutique." I hurriedly continued. "My name is Trixie Montgomery, and I write for *Georgia By the Way.*

Her face lit up with instant recognition and her attitude changed faster than a chameleon's colors. "Follow me and we'll go somewhere we can talk undisturbed. Let me tell Katy, my assistant, and I'll be right with you." She tucked the polishing cloth back into her belt and disappeared through a door marked "Employees Only."

I plopped in a rocker to ease the pain in my leg. Relief washed a cool wave over my throbbing knee. Rocking back and forth it occurred to me she didn't seem upset her ex-husband was dead.

"Let's go back to my office." Miranda interrupted my thoughts. She led the way, careening through a maze of furniture.

Her so-called office could easily pass for a closet. I felt sure it had been one at one time.

I started with questions concerning her business, and moved on to her position with the Historical Society. I took notes and recorded our conversation.

Time passed quickly. I needed to pick up Dee Dee shortly, and I hadn't even addressed John Tatum, so I charged ahead like a bull in a daisy patch.

"Thanks so much for your time today, Miranda." I smiled, closing my little book. "I'm sorry to hear of your husband's death."

Her angelic smile faded. "My ex-husband." She stood up and bee-lined for the door. "I don't see what this has to do with your article."

Think fast Trixie. "Joyce mentioned it when she told me about your antique business. That the man who was murdered yesterday was your *ex*-husband." I wouldn't make the mistake of saying "husband" again.

She froze, her hand on the knob.

"I have an ex-husband, too. By the sound of it, I'd guess we have some things in common. My husband and I were married twenty years before he decided to trade me in for a newer model. As far as I'm concerned, he blew his chances of ever repairing our relationship—not that he ever tried."

She jerked the door back; the little bell almost flew off, tinkling angrily.

Before I stepped out, I couldn't help myself and climbed out on a limb. "Uh, is that what John Tatum did to you?"

I'll swanny, I saw smoke come from her ears. Her pretty face scrunched up and she balled her fists. At that moment, I imagined that Miranda Tatum was capable of murder in the first degree.

CHAPTER TEN

You want a reaction?" Venom spewed when she spoke. "This is it. That no-good, son of a gun got what he deserved. I did everything to make that man happy. Was that enough? No, it wasn't. He had to have an affair with his so-called secretary. I'd wager she couldn't turn on an electric typewriter, much less a computer. You know the type, don't you?"

I certainly did. My curls danced as I nodded my head in agreement, encouraging her to continue.

"Not only did he mess around with her, he got her pregnant. You'd think he was old enough to know where babies come from. When he found out, he dropped her like a hot potato. Claimed the baby wasn't even his." Her lower lip quivered.

There were no words to console her. I knitted my hands and waited her out.

"I heard she was mad enough to kill him when he denied he was the father. He told her he'd marry her when our divorce finalized. He didn't marry her, and he abandoned her with a baby to bring up by herself. I don't know who hates him more, me or his mistress. Is that enough reaction for you?" Her creamy cheeks had turned a mottled pink. Her murderous, green-eyed stare dared me to defy her anger.

A knock broke the tiny roomed tension. A woman poked her head around the corner.

Before I could react, in stepped a bountifully rotund woman dressed in a bright orange sweater, covered with glittering black sequined cats.

"Is there anything in here for sale?" She screwed her lips at us and decided there wasn't. "I guess not. Sorry." She scooted out. Her garish holiday ensemble reminded me I needed to check on Dee Dee.

"I'm sorry if I triggered painful memories. I'm sure this hasn't been easy for you." I figured since Miranda was mad at me, why not go ahead and stick my foot all the way in. "By the way, I do have one more question for you. Where were you last night?"

One of Nana's quotes rang in my ears at the change in Miranda's amicable expression. "Never believe blondes, natural or bottled, are as dumb as the jokes suggest."

"Thanks, Ms. Montgomery." Miranda regained her composure, and the veil of our newfound camaraderie shred in two. "I think our interview is over." She flung an arm into the doorway, indicating she meant what she said. "I trust you've got all you need for your article, and the rest is none of your business."

"I appreciate the time you've given me, and I'll be sure and notify you when it's published." I dug in my purse for a business card and handed it to her. "Please call me if you think of anything else you'd like to add." *Like, maybe you killed your ex-husband.*

Information swirled in my mind like leaves in a whirlwind. I hurried down the street, and the more I thought about it, the more her hostile attitude disturbed me. There was little doubt in my mind that the angelic Miranda harbored enough hate within to kill her ex-husband. Not only did Miranda have a motive for killing John, but his girlfriend did, too.

I knew what it felt like to be an outraged ex first hand. But I never imagined actually carrying out my fantasies. Was either one of these women capable of murder?

I stepped inside the sheriff's department and an office door opened. Dee Dee rushed out with Sheriff Wheeler close behind. Her expression brightened as soon as she saw me.

The sheriff followed her to where I stood. "Ms. Lamont, thank you for your time. We'll let you know if we need anything more." He turned towards me with a lingering gaze, "How are you doing Ms. Montgomery?"

"P-please call me Trixie," I reminded him, pushing down that over-powering urge to flirt when I was around him. With his good looks and southern charm, he was probably used to women fawning over him. After all, he was the enemy, and everyone knows you don't fraternize with the enemy. *Or was it, "keep your friends close, and your enemies closer?"*

He rewarded me with a beatific grin, and I continued, "Considering the circumstances, I could be worse." I plowed right ahead. "By the way, have you started looking at other suspects? I have reason to believe John Tatum made more than one enemy along the way. Some say that having an angry ex-wife and an angrier ex-girlfriend could present a sticky situation."

"And how did you come up with this information?" He looked me square in the eyes. "I hope you're not interfering in this investigation." He placed a warm, but warning hand on my shoulder and guided me toward the door. "You have my pledge I'll follow any and every lead I believe important to this case. That's what I'm trained to do."

We said our good-byes, and I firmly shut the door - maybe a bit firmer than necessary.

"Oh Trixie, it was awful." Dee Dee pulled out a ragged tissue from her pocket and dabbed at her eyes.

"Sheriff Wheeler and Deputy Ray grilled me, then they left me alone with that GBI man." The tissue was used for a makeshift hanky. She blew her nose and discarded it in a nearby trashcan. "Good grief, I didn't even know the dead guy."

I squeezed Dee Dee's arm for reassurance. "I think they're trying to make the puzzle pieces fit where they don't belong."

"That makes sense," Dee Dee nodded. "I might have discovered a reason why the sheriff wants to solve this case in such a hurry. I over-heard him talking to Agent Cornwall. The sheriff wants to retire soon and run for Mayor. He said, 'It'll be great to have this case closed by the time I leave office.' Can you believe that?" Dee Dee plopped down on a bench and removed her shoe. She shook it and a small pebble fell out.

I sat down beside her and people watched a long moment, gathering my thoughts. The crowd was growing and, shortly, the streets and sidewalks would be wall-to-wall people. I leaned my cane on the wooden bench, but it slid off and onto the pavement. I let it lay there for the time being.

We sat quietly watching the throng of excited passers-by. Was Jake Wheeler trying to pin Tatum's murder on Dee Dee? I didn't want to believe this attractive man would use Dee Dee as a scapegoat.

"Dee, it makes perfect sense." I poked her knee and she started. "No wonder he focused on you from the beginning. In his mind, this was an open and shut case from the time he saw you standing there with Tatum's blood on your hands. It doesn't hurt that you're an out-of-towner. Don't want to offend too many locals who vote."

This put a new perspective on the situation. Would the sheriff cover all the bases? Possibly, but I wasn't taking any chances. I had to continue my own investigation.

CHAPTER ELEVEN

My stomach growled like a lion, and we both laughed. "Come on Dee. Let's get something to eat."

"That's the best offer I've had all day," Dee Dee rooted in her gigantean shoulder bag. She pulled out her favorite "Ruby's Red" lipstick, painted on a fresh coat, stood up, and readjusted her clothes. "Let's walk around the square and see if we can find a nice café that isn't too crowded."

The smell of funnel cake and other fried foods, along with the squeals of children in the park, bombarded my senses. Smiles and excitement glowed on the faces of the tourists. I fought the little stab of jealousy mixed with a scoop of anger, thinking, *If Dee Dee wasn't under a cloud of suspicion, we'd be smiling, too.*

We decided on a cute little sandwich shop: The Victorian Tea Room. The motif catered to women, and I blinked at the ladies in large hats sipping from bone china and nibbling on crustless sandwiches on the other side of the plate glass window.

"Would you look at this? Isn't it unique, Trix?" Dee Dee fingered a veiled hat on the wall, obviously itching to try it on.

"I don't think I've ever seen a tea room quite like this." Old-fashioned hats and shawls hung from the walls with an invitation to wear them. A few of the guests had donned the fancy attire and were taking pictures of each other. Tables decked in lace tablecloths were covered with hand painted china, reminiscent of my grandmother's house.

A cute young girl in her early twenties, short brown hair streaked with purple, and earrings in places I wouldn't dream of piercing, showed us to our table. The menu consisted of food destined to win a girl's heart, and stomach. Sandwiches, fresh fruit, scones and muffins made up the lunch cuisine. We chose the chicken salad sandwich on a croissant. For dessert: fresh strawberries covered in brandy sauce and topped with whipped cream.

Hot Cinnamon Spice and Peach tea sat on the table in individual teapots. The cinnamon flavor floated in the air like magnolia in the evening. My nostrils filled with the heavenly scent as we doctored our tea, and then settled back to talk.

Before the swish of a lamb's tail, the waitress brought our sandwiches. The crust on the croissant resembled homemade piecrust; it did a buttery dance across my taste buds. We managed to enjoy our food, despite being stressed.

I started on my fresh fruit, savoring every bite, when the jingle of the doorbell drew my attention towards the door. "Oh, no!" I whispered.

As soon as Miranda walked in, the chef barreled through the kitchen doors and hurried to her side. They conferred for a moment, and then he went back into the kitchen. She stood ramrod straight as she gazed around the room. Her face gave away nothing, that was, until she caught my eye. Her fiery eyes shot daggers.

The chef returned, laden with several bags, and handed them to her. She turned on her heels and clicked out of the café without so much as a nod.

"Good grief. If looks could kill, I believe we'd be dead." Dee Dee turned around in her lattice chair from watching the scene. "Who was that?"

"That my dear, is Miranda Tatum. John Tatum's ex-wife."

"The infamous Miranda." Several heads turned our way.

"Shhh. Let's finish our dessert and I'll fill you in later." We finished eating and headed for the bathroom—the place that got us into trouble in the first place. Dee Dee forever needed to go to the bathroom. I'd tried to get her to tell her doctor, like they suggest on the television commercial, but she didn't see it as a problem. I'd bet now she'd visit him as soon as we got back home.

We stepped back into the busy street and were immediately engulfed by a sea of people. I had to holler to get her attention. "Let's go over to the Gold Museum and see if we can wheedle some information from Teresa."

"Why?"

"Oh, I don't know. Because I like to wheedle people?" I smiled to let her know I was only kidding.

"Huh?" Her face was blank. Unusual for Dee Dee, she missed the joke. The investigation must have really gotten under her skin.

"Well, if we're going to find out who killed John Tatum, we'll have to create a list of suspects."

Dee Dee stopped abruptly.

"Whoa. I almost ran into you," I laughed.

"Well, with all my cushioning back there, it wouldn't hurt you. Where did you get the crazy notion to snoop for suspects?" She stood firm, not moving an inch.

"Do you have any better ideas? You said yourself that Sheriff Wheeler needed to close this case as soon as possible. Joyce said that there are a lot of people who had reason to want Tatum dead. We can find out who they are, tell the sheriff, and let him follow-up."

"Well, put that way it doesn't sound like a bad idea. I don't want you to put yourself in danger for my sake." Dee Dee adjusted her shoulder bag and we continued walking.

We elbowed our way through the throng of people. Several of the festival booths seemed to call our names so we stopped to check out their colorful knick-knacks. We moved with the crowd until we reached the end of the street.

We stood at the corner, admiring the fancy, horse-drawn carriage providing rides around the square. As it turned, it nearly ran over us. We jumped out of the way. I felt something squishy under my foot. Let me tell you, those horsey diapers don't work as well as you'd think.

I spied some grassy lawns around the museum. "Come on. Let's go over there so I can clean my shoes."

Dee Dee belly laughed.

It was good to hear, even if it was at my expense. "Thanks a heap, these are my new Rockports."

"I'm sorry. I can't help it. You should have seen the look on your face," she managed to sputter.

I grabbed her arm and pulled her towards the museum. By that time I was laughing, too. But as we got closer, my mirth slowly died from my lips.

Teresa might not be an easy mark for my line of questioning, but for Dee Dee's sake, we had to try.

CHAPTER TWELVE

H ello, ladies. What brings you back to the museum?" Teresa's thin smile looked forced and unnatural when we walked in.

"Can we talk to you for a minute?"

Teresa adjusted the badge on her uniform. "For a minute. They've finished taking down the crime scene tape. I want to make sure the mining room is cleaned up. I don't want any of our visitors upset by blood stains." She looked directly at us with displeasure, and I didn't blame her.

"Let's go to my office." She led the way.

"I'm so sorry this happened. This must be such an inconvenience for you, especially during the busiest time of the year."

"Not to mention the embarrassment it has caused. One of the most influential men in Dahlonega was murdered on my watch, and I was up for a promotion." She muttered under her breath. The softly spoken words sounded something like, "I guess I can kiss that good-bye."

"Umm, look on the bright side. It might boost the tourist traffic today. You know how people possess a morbid curiosity." A nervous giggle escaped my lips.

Teresa turned and gave me a funny look as Dee Dee poked me in the ribs.

"I hope you don't think Dee Dee murdered Mr. Tatum. It was a case of being in the wrong place at the wrong time—"

"Look, Trixie," Teresa interrupted. "I'm not sure what to think. I know for a fact that John Tatum had more than one enemy. He made some thoroughly bad decisions - others came with the territory of possessing enough power to say 'yea' or 'nay' to someone in need." She pointed to some chairs, indicating for us to sit down.

"I could use some help locating some of these people, and Joyce said no one knows the people or the town as well as you do." I leaned toward Teresa, now seated behind her desk. "I heard John and Miranda Tatum had a messy divorce." I searched her face for a reaction but saw no change. I continued. "Could you tell me about John's girlfriend? Give me her name and how to get in contact with her?"

"Look, I shouldn't." She looked from me to Dee Dee, then back to me. "But if my best friend was in trouble, I'd do the same thing. Promise you won't do anything but ask questions, and leave the rest up to Sheriff Wheeler. One person's dead already."

I nodded.

Dee Dee spoke up. "I'll promise for both of us." She squinched her eyes and glared at me.

Teresa's shoulders relaxed and I thought, *Way to go Dee Dee*. But I had every intention of doing whatever was necessary to prove Dee Dee's innocence.

"What's her name, and where can we find her?" I handed paper and pen to Dee Dee so she could play secretary.

"Her family name is Dalton. Sueleigh Dalton. She lives with her kin several miles outside of town. You might be able to find her whole family at the festival today. They run a food stand every year during Gold Rush Days and she helps them out." Teresa scooted back in her chair and adjusted her badge. Again.

"I can't thank you enough. You wait and see; you have my word. When this is over, Dee Dee will be exonerated." I gave Dee Dee a big smile and touched her shoulder. I talked tough, but could I make it happen? I had to believe I could, with some help from above.

"I don't know why, but for some reason, I believe you." Teresa tapped her teeth, as if considering her options. "There's one more person you might be interested in."

Dee Dee and I both belted out, "Who?"

"A couple of years ago, there was a robbery at the Tatum place. Tubby

Hawkins, a local teenager, broke into Tatum's home, but he didn't make it out alive. He was a known trouble maker and had a gun in his possession, so no charges were filed against Tatum, but John killed the boy, all the same." She shifted around in her office chair, obviously unsettled by the events.

"The Hawkins family was outraged and vowed revenge on Tatum. Tommy Hawkins, Tubby's older brother, was the most vocal. He went around town telling everyone that Tatum had better watch his back. No one was going to kill his brother and get away with it."

"Wow!" Dee Dee sat on the edge of her chair.

"This could be a big break." My wheels already turning, I glanced at Dee Dee, who was furiously writing names on her note pad. I turned back to Teresa. "I wonder if the sheriff's looked at this angle. This Tommy character should be at the top of the suspect list."

"Remember, you didn't hear any of this from me."

"Of course," I nodded, attempting to make my expression the model of discretion. "One last thing: I've heard the sheriff's going to retire? He could solve this case by blaming the most obvious suspect instead of investigating other leads. It would be mighty convenient for him to focus on Dee Dee."

She stood and placed fists to her hips. "I've known Jake Wheeler for years, and I believe he'll follow any lead he thinks important." She drew herself up. "Now I've got to inspect the rooms so we can open."

Dee Dee and I knew the way out, and it was obvious she wanted us to go, pronto!

CHAPTER THIRTEEN

Teresa retrieved some papers and started to leave.

"Oh, Teresa!" Dee Dee begged, in her not so subtle way. "I need to use the ladies room if you don't mind."

I wasn't surprised.

Teresa's eyes shot open like a cat whose tail had been stepped on. She wasted no time ushering us out the door.

"Well, ladies, I hate to be rude, but...No, I'm going to be honest. I don't hate to be rude. I can't take a chance on anything else happening while you two are loose in the museum. There's a public restroom across the square." She had me by one arm and Dee Dee by the other as she led us out. She stood, still as a statue, until we walked down the outside steps.

I'm sure my, "thanks for the information" was lost in the wind as she turned and hurried back into the museum.

"Well, I can't blame her," Dee Dee said.

"Me neither." I replied as we stood, deciding what to do next.

"Our list grows longer." Dee Dee thrust her notepad in my face as she hot stepped toward the public restroom.

I reviewed our growing list of suspects while we stood in line at the facilities. Afterwards, we decided to stop in a quaint little ice cream and pastry shop for an afternoon pick-me-up. Country themed gifts, coffee cups painted with flowers and butterflies, Christmas wreaths, antique jewelry and home decor fragrances, and heavenly scented candles lined the shelves along the walls. We looked for a minute, then found a corner table and placed our order.

I slid on my reading glasses and waggled my fingers. "Bring out the suspect list and let's go over it."

Dee Dee brought out the tablet faster than a magician pulling a rabbit out of a hat. "So far, we have Miranda Tatum. A woman scorned is one to be contended with. Her husband's betrayal has left deep scars that haven't healed yet. I should know." I wondered, prayed, that the time would come when I'd be able to think of Wade without that sharp stab of pain.

Dee Dee gave me a little shake. "Girl, where did you go? You looked like you took a trip to La-La Land again. From what you've told me, Sueleigh Dalton wasn't any happier with Tatum's treatment of women. It seems like he used women and tossed them away like disposable commodities. Use them and lose them." She rolled her eyes. "Men!"

I nodded. "Don't forget Tommy Hawkins. Teresa said he didn't hide his hatred for Tatum. He told the whole town he was going to kill him."

Dee Dee pointed at his name written on the page. "You heard Teresa. The Hawkins are meaner than a mama bear protecting her cubs. Good grief, she refused to tell you where they live."

The waitress slid our dishes onto the Formica. "Anything else?"

"No thanks," I smiled at her before picking up my spoon.

"I don't think we need to mess with them." Dee Dee scooped into her whipped cream as the waitress walked away.

"True, but we can find it ourselves." I savored a mouthful of my ice cream and sighed. "Speaking of Harv."

"We weren't speaking of Harv, Goofy." Dee Dee poked her spoon at me.

I laughed. "I know, but he popped into my head, and I felt like pulling your string." I did love to tease Dee Dee. And she loved to tease me.

I noticed a lonely tear running down Dee Dee's face. "I'm, sorry Dee; I didn't mean to hurt your feelings." Man, I felt like a jerk.

She sniffed. "No, it's not that. You didn't hurt my feelings. I miss my babies." she was referring to her furry babies; all five of them. I never understood the attraction to cats—I'm a dog woman myself. But the love for her cats is as strong as the love I have for my dog, Bouncer.

The tears streamed down her face. As any woman knows, crying plus make-up equals raccoon eyes. Dee Dee dabbed her napkin at her cheeks.

"I'm sorry, sweetie; I'm sure you miss them." I squeezed her hand, knowing she was now upset about more than her cats.

"Its times like this I want to wring Gary's neck for going and dying on me. I don't want to face this all alone. I'm scared." She rubbed her eyes, enlarging the black circles of smeared mascara.

"You aren't alone, Dee. I'm here. And, as you always tell me, we are never really alone. We have someone who loves us unconditionally." We shared a long, stuttering glance, and hand-hugged. She sniffed and wiped her nose.

"You're right. I need to practice what I preach. Come on. Let's go back to the room for a while. I want to freshen up."

We left desserts half-eaten and paid our check. I led the way back to the Dahlonega Inn.

When I keyed the door, it pushed open, unlocked. "Did you remember to lock the door?" I whispered to Dee Dee.

She shook her head, eyes wide.

Inside, I heard shuffling, then the squeak of a mattress. Someone was in the room!

CHAPTER FOURTEEN

I slowly pushed the door open, praying protection from whatever awaited us. And there, sitting on the corner of my bed, dressed in jogging pants and matching pull-over, sat my great aunt.

"NANA!" My heart jackhammered. "What in the world are you doing here?"

"I'm glad to see you, too, Missy," my white-haired aunt shot a smile, green eyes peering from behind her glasses.

Dee Dee concocted an excellent excuse and left me to handle the situation alone, rushing past us for the ladies room.

"Nana, how did you travel all the way to Dahlonega? I gave her a hug and stepped back, hands on my hips, waiting on her explanation. "And this had better be good."

"Beau."

Beau? Nana's answer shocked my socks off.

"He's over at the sheriff's department right this minute, looking into the murder investigation. Isn't this something? How in the world did you get mixed up in this?"

Nana bounced on her seat, up and down. I hoped she wasn't testing it out for that night.

"Nana, I'm the one asking the questions."

"You can get off your high horse, Missy. I'm sure you're surprised to see me, but that's no reason to get sassy with me."

Nana didn't seem fazed by my authoritative tone.

"I'm sorry, Nana. I'm just surprised to see you. What in the name of Jehoshaphat made you and Beau decide to come to Dahlonega?"

I sat on the edge of the other bed, no longer able to stand. My knee throbbed. Dee Dee came back in and plopped down beside me.

"Now, don't go and get mad at Beau," Nana said. "I threatened to find another ride if he didn't bring me. Remember, Beau's a deputy sheriff. Who better to help you? I thought you'd be happy." Tears sparkled in the corner of Nana's eyes. Nana didn't cry often. She'd been brought up during an era where living was anything but easy. There had been precious little time to cry then.

"Don't cry, Nana. We'll work this out." I hugged her. She brightened up a little too quickly.

Dee Dee asked, "How did you know about the murder, Nana?"

"I happened to answer the phone at the same time Betty Jo did and overheard part of Trixie's conversation." She looked me straight in the face and dared me to say different.

"I knew it! I had this weird feeling when I was on the phone talking with Mama. Nana, you eavesdropped." I crossed my arms.

"That's not true." She sniffed, as if daring me to think her intent malicious. "When I heard you crying, I couldn't hang up the phone."

Her features softened. I melted.

"You're here now. Let's call Mama and make sure she knows you're all right. She does know where you are?"

"Of course she does," Nana responded with indignation. It was a miracle. She seemed to have successfully erased her memory of all the times her antics resulted in worrying Mama.

"I'm not even going to ask you how you managed to talk her into letting you come." Mama, bless her heart, needed the time away from Nana. She loved her, without a doubt. Caring for Nana was tougher than a big-bootied woman struggling to pull on a pair of spandex pants.

"Good. We're wasting time. I'm here to help. What can I do?" Nana picked up the hooded jacket to her jogging outfit and looped her arm through her pocketbook.

"Nana, I'm sorry, but I can't let you get involved." I brainstormed on ways to convince Nana to return home as I tried to pry her jacket from her hands. She wasn't having it. She pried back.

"We appreciate your concern Nana, but I think we have the situation under control. Beau's come all the way to Dahlonega to help, and he'll straighten things out." I prayed he could.

Nana fluttered her lashes. "Can you believe it? A hunk with brains. They just don't make 'em like that anymore. If I were a little younger, I'd go for Beau. I'd catch him, too." She placed her jacket and pocketbook on the bed, and fluffed her hair. The she winked at us. "You're right Trix, Beau can take care of it."

I glanced over at Dee Dee. I pleaded with my eyes, begging for her help. She responded by shrugging her shoulders. In other words, "you're on your own, honey."

I pressed forward. "You're right, Nana. Beau's a hunk, and I agree he's smart enough to help Dee Dee. Why don't we call Mama and tell her you're coming home now that you've seen everything's fine?"

She looked at me like I'd grown horns, and I glared back.

A knock at the door broke our stare down. Closest to the door, I opened it. In front of me stood a beautiful sight:Beau, looking like he'd stepped out of a Wrangler jeans ad. Without thinking, I gave him a big hug. Warmth flowed through me when he hugged back. Embarrassed, I pulled back.

When Beau wiped a lone tear from my cheek, a tingle of electricity ran through my body. I couldn't remember a time, since my divorce, when my protective armor had been penetrated. I welcomed the warm feeling.

Beau cleared his throat. "I had a thorough talk with Jake, and I believe he's doing what he can to solve—"

"Are you sure we're talking about the same Sheriff Wheeler? The one who's hounding Dee Dee?"

"Trixie, your mama taught you better than to interrupt someone," Nana intoned from the bed.

I ignored Nana's words and Beau's smile. "Furthermore, we think he's using her for a scapegoat. He's retiring at the end of the year."

Dee Dee nodded in agreement, "Yes, and he's running for mayor."

Beau turned from her to me, and butterflies fluttered at the full force of his attention. "I feel confident Jake's doing his job. He's not going to divulge details of the case with civilians. I wouldn't, either."

That made me wonder what the sheriff had told him. "So is there anything I *can* know?"

His lips twitched. "He mentioned several persons of interest other than Dee Dee." Beau had my full attention. "But you have to admit it didn't look good when the rangers found Dee Dee standing over Tatum. She immediately became a person of interest."

Dee Dee snorted. "Like I would kill anyone."

Beau shrugged. "Sheriff Wheeler wouldn't know that, and he wouldn't be doing a thorough job if he didn't look into you."

I glared at him. "Whose side are you on?" I should have cut him a break, seeing as he'd spent all that time in a car with Nana, but I couldn't help myself.

He sighed, and pulled up a chair.

"I guess you're right. They're not going to share information with the suspect and her friend," Dee Dee said.

Beau took off his Stetson and ran his long fingers through his hair. Then he dropped the bomb. "Now, for the bad news."

CHAPTER FIFTEEN

I received a call from my partner, Deputy Crowe." Beau spun the Stetson slowly. "Last year, our department worked on a case involving stolen cattle. Crowe said they've arrested a man in the next county, and he's asking for me. There's a good chance he's involved in stealin' cattle from the local farmers. He's refusing to talk to anyone else. I've got to go back."

Beau brushed back his thick hair and rubbed his chin before he replaced his hat. He stood up.

I panicked. Our only chance to get Nana back home was going to leave. "Uh, Beau. Since you're going back anyway, why don't you give Nana a ride home?" I grabbed her jacket and pocketbook and shoved them towards him.

He shoved the items back at me and opened the door. With a wide sweep of his hand he gestured for me to go outside. He followed me and shut the door behind him.

"I'm sorry, but it just ain't gonna' happen today."

Disbelief flooded me in waves. Had I heard him right? He refused to take her home? Equally bad, our liaison to Sheriff Wheeler was getting ready to walk out the door.

I swayed a bit, and Beau reached out and steadied me. It hit me again: a surge of electricity traveled from my head to my toes at the touch of his hand.

"I'm really sorry, but I have to go back immediately, and I won't be able to take Nana home. The guy could change his mind any minute." He loosened his hold on me and, when I didn't fall flat on my face, he let go.

Making a scene wouldn't change a thing, and I didn't want Beau to leave on a bad note. His friendship meant too much to me. "You're right Beau. I know how important this is. You need to go back as soon as possible." I stalled for more time. "Something has been bothering me. No one's talking about the money scattered around John Tatum's body. Do you think blackmail might be involved?"

"Blackmail is a possibility. A well known figure like Tatum makes a good target for blackmail."

My hopes soared. "I've talked with some of the locals, and they've given me a few leads. I can request a follow-up interview. Ask them more questions." I couldn't wait to start.

He took his hat off and slapped it against his leg, face drawn into a scowl. "Trixie, let the sheriff take care of this. I have confidence he'll do his job, and...it could be dangerous."

As touched as I was that Beau cared, I couldn't agree.

Beau put his hat back on his head and leaned his face in toward mine. "Promise me."

I crossed my fingers behind my back. "Okay, I'll stay out of trouble." I didn't promise not to question anyone.

He waited. I kept my fingers crossed. I feared they might become permanently stuck that way.

Then he backed up with a sigh. "I guess that's the best I'll get from you."

Beau was wise enough to let it drop. We stepped back inside and he said his goodbyes to Nana and Dee Dee. He kissed Nana on the cheek. A prick of jealously stung me. These new feelings for him confused me. Maybe it was the mountain air.

He turned back to me. "You've got my cell number; call me if you need anything. I can get in touch with Sheriff Wheeler right away. All right?" He waited for my answer.

"I'll call if I need to. Thanks for coming."

He left and I waved one last time from the doorway. A surge of sadness washed over me. I shut the door and turned around.

Dee Dee and Nana had their heads close together, deep in conversation. They stopped mid-sentence. I wondered if I were the subject of their cozy little chat.

"We were discussing sleeping arrangements," Nana said. "Would either of you want to share a bed with me?" She chuckled. She knew good and well we didn't. "Just kidding. Why don't we call those nice people down at the front desk and ask them if they have a roll-a-way bed."

I glanced around the cramped room, wondering where we'd put a roll-a-way bed. I sent up a prayer for help. I didn't hear a voice from heaven, but I did feel a sense of peace. Where there's a will, there's a way, and Nana would find it.

"Trixie, please call them. I do believe I feel a nap sneaking up." A yawn confirmed Nana's exhaustion.

I pulled back the covers. "Dee Dee and I have a few errands we need to run. You can use my bed for your nap. I'll stop at the desk and ask for a roll-away."

"What errands?" Dee Dee shrugged and wore a blank look.

"You know, Dee Dee, the errands we discussed this morning." I raised a brow.

"Oh, yeah. I remember." She spoke loud enough to wake the dead. "Nana, can we do anything for you before we go?"

"No dear. You two go ahead. When you get back we can get some supper. Beau and I had burgers and fries in the car."

Nana unzipped her overnight bag. I was amazed at how conveniently sharp Nana's mind could be.

"Dee Dee, grab my jacket please. It's much cooler out." We donned our jackets and I retrieved my cane where it leaned against the wall. This trip had convinced me it would not be much longer before surgery was necessary. I picked up my camera and we shut the door, leaving Nana to her unpacking.

"What errands were you talking about, Trix?"

"I want to see if we can locate Sueleigh Dalton. Teresa said her family run one of the booths on the square."

"She was John Tatum's girlfriend, right?" Dee Dee asked.

"Yes. And she had a baby by him and then he denied being the father." I looked at Dee Dee. "I believe that could be a recipe for murder."

CHAPTER SIXTEEN

She laughed at my pun, but stopped short when she realized I was serious. "You're right, Trixie. Murders have been committed for a lot less. Why, the sheriff thinks I killed Tatum over a silly argument. It doesn't make sense to me. Just because I stood over Tatum holding the murder weapon…." A sheepish look claimed her face. "Oh, yeah. Holding the murder weapon doesn't bode well for me, does it?" Her countenance fell.

It hurt to witness my friend in so much pain. With Dee Dee's freedom on the line, I was determined to support her. She had supported me during my divorce and I wanted to be there for her.

"Come on," I pulled her towards a booth surrounded by tourists. We waited in line for a funnel cake, a tasty treat made of deep-fried dough, covered with powdered sugar. I often thought just inhaling the aroma could add pounds to my figure—so I planned to order one for Dee Dee as well as one for me. If I were going to gain weight, I refused to gain alone.

I squeezed up to the counter before Dee Dee.

"Hey lady, can I help you?" The man behind the counter wiped his hands on his greasy apron.

What the heck. It was for a good cause. "Yes, we'll take two funnel cakes please, and lots of powdered sugar." He handed one to me and yelled for another one. "Can you tell me where I can find the Dalton's booth?"

"Sure. They run the Backyard Bar-b-que. It's across the street and down a ways to the left. That'll be six fifty." He accepted my change and barked, "Next!"

I had been dismissed. I moved over to let a less than petite woman elbow her way to the counter.

I handed Dee Dee her funnel cake and she unwound a long curl of the doughy treat. "This'll be good for a quick energy boost." She looked cute with white powder all around her mouth. "Where are we going?"

My mouth full, I pointed across the street. We headed in that direction, holding the flimsy plates steady as we savored our treats.

The Dalton's booth was easy to find. Another long line flowed into the street. Eating must be the main event at Gold Rush Days.

"Looks like we might have to buy a sandwich, too." I brushed my sticky mouth and threw the trash in a plastic-lined bin.

"Yes, it does." Dee Dee added, tossing her plate in, as well.

As we approached the booth, I saw several people working inside. Two men and two women danced around each other as they filled orders. I wondered which one was Sueleigh.

"Next!"

"I'll take two sandwiches and two Cokes, please." As the man handed me our food, I asked which lady was Sueleigh.

"Neither one. Sueleigh is my daughter. Why ya' asking?" His words were clipped and his tone unfriendly.

That would never do. I set on my reporter's grin, and introduced myself. "I write for a historical magazine, and I want to interview her. Teresa Duncan, over at the Gold Museum, recommended I talk with Sueleigh about Gold Rush Days." All right, we all stretch the truth at times. I prayed the end justified the means.

"Teresa. Why didn't ya' say so?" A smile softened his gruff exterior. "Sueleigh is driving the horse carriage for me today. You can catch her over there." He pointed to the square. I glanced at my shoe. Unfortunately, I was familiar with the horse carriage.

"Thanks, thanks a lot." I don't think he heard me. He'd moved on to the next hungry customer. I turned around and bumped into Dee Dee.

"I heard. I guess we're on our way to the carriage ride?" She grabbed a Coke and took a long drink.

"Let's find somewhere to sit." We sat in silence, on a bench facing the square. It was the perfect setting for people watching.

I'm a firm believer that if your self-confidence is in danger of waning, you should go to the mall and people watch. God made humans in all different sizes, shapes, colors, and personalities. The bottom line is, we're all pretty much made from the same pattern.

"People watching again?" Dee Dee asked, slurping her drink.

"Isn't it odd how the Lord made people in all shapes and sizes?"

We watched a family of four, one kid in braces, the second with a gap-toothed smile that showed he'd be next.

"Ever notice how the beautiful people on television are never at the farmer's markets?"

"Or the mall." Dee Dee nodded. "And their beauty has been enhanced, at that!"

I agreed, having participated in this activity many times after my divorce. My self-esteem was then at an all time low. It had taken me a great deal of contemplation to realize he hadn't strayed because of my looks or my self-esteem. He had strayed because of his *own* lack of self-esteem, disguised as an overblown ego. He still didn't understand, and I wasn't making any bets he ever would. That was okay. I'd discovered that I needed to spend my limited energy on me and let God take care of Wade.

As I sat thinking, the clippity-clop of a horse pulling a carriage sounded behind us. We turned to see a stunning redhead high on the driver's seat. She wasn't alone. A man, who looked vaguely familiar, sat next to her.

I poked Dee Dee in the ribs.

"Ouch." She rubbed her side. "What did you do that for?"

"Look over there. See the man sitting next to the redhead?"

"Sure. What's so important about him you had to crack my rib?"

"That looks like Leroy, Joyce's nephew. What do you think he's doing talking with Sueleigh Dalton? That guy gives me the creeps. I thought I was going to wet my pants when he snuck up on me last night." I wadded up my sandwich wrapper and threw it in a nearby garbage can.

"Don't exaggerate, Trix. You said he was making his nightly rounds. It's no wonder you were edgy last night after the horrible day we'd been through."

I knew she was trying her best to convince me that I was wrong, but it wasn't working. "Dee Dee, there's something in my gut. I just can't put my finger on it. To see him talking with Sueleigh adds fuel to the fire. Some coincidence if you ask me. Come on; let's buy a ticket for the carriage ride. I'm going to find out one way or the other what he's up to."

CHAPTER SEVENTEEN

When the carriage turned the corner, we were next in line. I glanced over at Dee Dee. "Close your mouth before a fly takes up residence in there."

I knew what caused her laxity of the jaw. Even from a distance, I had to work hard to avert my stare and avoid taking in the whole picture. I knew why Tatum fell hard for Sueleigh. In fact, I could understand why any breathing male, regardless of age, might be attracted to her. A tight pale lavender sweater accentuated the largest set of manmade boobs I'd ever seen.

She wore her long, fiery red hair flowing down her back. Enough make up covered her face to qualify for a walking advertisement. No doubt, many a head had turned to get a second look at the combination of ample chest, red hair, and painted face.

"She'll never have to worry about falling flat on her face." Dee Dee chuckled at her bad joke.

"Shhhh! Act natural. Here she comes."

Next thing I knew, Sueleigh Dalton looked our way. She pulled the reins back and a beautiful brown and white horse came to a stop. "Hi. You ladies ready?"

"Sure. Come on Dee Dee." I grabbed her and guided her to the back seat, and then I turned to Sueleigh and asked her if I could sit up front. "I've always wanted to sit up front with the driver."

"I don't usually let riders up front. It could be dangerous; if there's an accident, somebody might file a law suit because they fell off the wagon," she laughed.

I didn't want to miss a chance to get up close and personal with a suspect, so I blurted out what I hoped would entice her to break the rules. "What if I told you I'm interested in interviewing you for a magazine article? I write for *Georgia By the Way*, and I'm working on an article about Gold Rush Days. I'd like my assistant to take your picture. There's a good chance it could make the cover."

She whooshed her hair behind her back. "In that case, I don't think it would hurt this one time. Come on up." She eyed my cane with a quizzical expression. "Do you need me to help you up?"

"I think I can make it if you give me a hand." With a little grunting and groaning, Sueleigh managed to pull me up beside her. With a flick of the reins and a 'giddy up,' we started on our way.

"The man riding with you looked familiar. Does he work at the inn?"

"Oh, that's Leroy Roberts, the owner's nephew. He's a friend of mine. We go back a long way. As a matter of fact, we went to school together. We were discussing the murder of John Tatum. I guess you've heard about it?" She raised painted eyebrows in question. She pulled on a rein and the horse turned down a back street.

"Yes, we have. What did you discuss about the murder?"

Sueleigh emitted a high-pitched scream, making the horses ears flick back and forth. "Oh my Gosh!" she exclaimed. "I know who you are. You're the lady that killed John."

"That's not true," I said. I turned around to see if Dee Dee had heard. She seemed oblivious as she watched the scenery. I gave her one of my most charming smiles and continued.

"What I mean is, it wasn't anyone I know. My friend Dee Dee has, however, been questioned by the sheriff about the murder of your ex-boyfriend."

"How did you know he was my ex-boyfriend?" She narrowed her gaze and pulled back on the leather straps. The horse slowed. For a minute, I thought she might stop and order us out.

"Okay." I held my hands up in surrender. "I really *am* a reporter, and

I'm working on a story about Gold Rush Days, but I'm also trying to help my best friend. I've been asking around town about anyone closely associated with Tatum. I have to help Dee Dee. The sheriff doesn't seem interested in looking for the real killer, so we've decided to find out who it is." I waited to see her reaction. When she didn't kick us out I continued. "We need your help," I pleaded.

Sympathy cooled her gaze. "Well, I know what it's like to have people look at you like you're really bad. But how can I help you?"

"Is it true you and John were involved?" I asked, even though I knew the answer.

"If you call having his child *involved*, yes we were. He broke my heart. John told me over and over that he'd divorce Miranda so we could get married." Tears glistened in her eyes and my heart softened—until I remembered it was another woman's husband she'd been involved with. I swallowed down my judgment and listened as she went on.

"I was so excited when I found out I was pregnant. I just knew he'd divorce Miranda, marry me, and give the baby a name. Boy, was I ever wrong." The words spewed from her painted mouth. "He not only fired me as his secretary; he stopped calling me. I tried to contact him over and over. He told me I'd better stop harassing him or he was going to get a restraining order. Can you believe that?" She pulled back on the reins to let a group of tourists pass. "A restraining order. On me! I was carrying his child, and he threatened to have me arrested if I didn't stop bothering him. He even suggested I do something about the pregnancy. I know I might not be the brightest light bulb in the room, but I would never harm my unborn child."

She moved up a notch in my book as the horse's hooves clip-clopped along the street. People pointed and waved. Kids begged their parents for a ride.

It dawned on me; Sueleigh had grown used to the finger pointing for all sorts of different reasons. No matter what the circumstances, this woman had been wronged. Through it all, she had protected her unborn child.

Sueleigh continued. "After that, I stopped contacting him. I didn't want anything to do with that man. I have a beautiful little girl, and I've been raising her myself, with some help from my parents. They were furious with John. Daddy wanted me to take him to court and make him pay child support. I thought about it, but knowing John's temper, I decided to let it go. I didn't want his money anyway."

Her voice dropped several levels. "There's other ways besides money to make someone pay." She looked straight ahead and concentrated on turning the horse down a lane.

Whether it was by bribery or murder, I suddenly believed she'd made him pay, and dearly at that.

CHAPTER EIGHTEEN

I 'm sorry about your misfortune. I've been told John touched a lot of people's lives, but not always for the best." I spied the Visitor's Center approaching and knew the ride was ending, and I'd almost forgotten the magazine interview. "Sueleigh, can we take another lap around? I want to ask you a few more questions. Uh, about the carriage rides."

"If there's no one waiting. You want more information about the horses? We train our own you know. My father has trained carriage horses for people all over the United States."

"Uh, yeah, that's interesting." I scribbled so she'd think I really cared about the horses, and glanced over my shoulder. DeeDee's fingers were steepled in prayer, her eyes closed and lips moving. I shouted to get her attention and made a circle with my hand indicating we were going another round. She gave me a little wave. "Uh, Sueleigh. Can you think of anything else that might help clear my friend's name?"

"Nope, I can't tell you anything else that would help." She smiled thin and even, more like a sneer under her carefully placed façade.

I could see continuing this line of questioning was pointless. Sueleigh had given me enough to confirm she had as much a reason to want Tatum dead as anyone. And, she'd added two more suspects to my list. John certainly didn't hold a special place in her parents' hearts, either.

"One more question. I'm looking for Tommy Hawkins. Do you

know where he lives?" I thought those Tammy Faye eyes would pop right out of her head.

"Everybody knows Tommy Hawkins. Look, you don't want to go out there. He's crazy. He used to go around town, drunk as a skunk, telling anyone who'd listen he was going to kill John for shooting his brother." Sueleigh pulled back on the reins at the stop, and the carriage slowed to a halt.

"I heard as much. I need to talk with him, though. It sounds like he had every reason to want John dead. Don't you agree?"

She bobbed her head in agreement, catching my bait. "Yeah, sure. But that doesn't mean you need to go out there. You're asking for trouble if you do."

"Please tell me where 'there' is. If it were your friend in trouble, wouldn't you want to help her?" I must have hit a chord on her heartstrings because I could see her expression soften.

"Don't say I didn't warn you. The Hawkins' are the meanest folks in these parts. Everyone says they run a still back up in the woods behind their house. They've made it clear they don't want anyone snooping around their property." Her blue-shadowed eyes widened as she spoke. "Are you familiar with Amicalola Falls?"

I nodded my head yes.

"That's the road you'll take. Go five miles out of town until you see the sign. Take a right, and go another ten miles or so and you'll see the entrance, but don't turn in. You're going to go past the entrance and down the road another three or four miles." She gestured each turn with her hands.

I jotted down the directions in haste. I hoped I'd be able to read them when the time came. Outside the carriage, I had Dee Dee take a few shots of Sueleigh, posing with her horse.

By the time we said good-bye, you'd have thought we were best friends. It didn't seem to dawn on her that I had asked her questions that could implicate her in a murder. Maybe she wasn't "the brightest bulb in the room," but I'd taken a liking to this girl and hoped she didn't have anything to do with Tatum's murder.

Dee Dee and I were beat, emotionally and physically, and I needed to get back to the inn and check on Nana. "Come on, assistant." I hobbled a few steps and Dee Dee took my elbow to help steady me. "Let's go see what trouble Nana's cooked up."

When I limped into the room, Nana sat up sharply.

"Missy, what's wrong with you? Is your knee acting up again? If it were me, I wouldn't wait to have surgery."

"It's not your knee they're going to cut open, Nana." I clipped, and regretted it. She was right, though. I had put it off much too long. My job required a lot of walking, so the condition wasn't going to get any better as time went by. I made a mental note to consult with the orthopedic surgeon when we got back home. Sooner than later I hoped.

Nana sat on a cot surrounded by an empty pizza box and a big bottle of Coke she'd had for lunch, and practically thrummed with the sugar coursing through her veins. "Well, do you see anything different?"

I assumed she was talking about the roll-away and not the food.

In the crowded room, the extra bed made it impossible to go to the bathroom without turning sideways. The small area had become a breeding ground for stubbed toes and bumped knees.

"And who will be sleeping on the cot, may I ask?"

Nana spoke up. "I don't mind sleeping on it. I'm tough."

Dee Dee glanced at me with raised eyebrows, then turned to Nana. "Nana! Don't be silly. I'll be glad to."

"Oh, good grief. I was kidding!" I sank down on the cot, squeaks filling the room, wires poking my backside. "Can't you guys take a little humor?"

"You most certainly will not. Your knee is killing you. I won't have you tossing and turning all night. You'll keep us awake," Dee Dee winked. She stood with her hands on her hips, looking as if she could take on the world. Who was I to argue? She needed a little control in her life. Since my knee hurt, it was a win-win situation.

"Ladies, let's save this for later. I'm hungry, and they're serving dinner now. You don't want to miss it, do you? Just let me get my pocketbook."

Dee Dee and I grabbed our purses, too, and together we maneuvered out of the door.

CHAPTER NINETEEN

The dining room held a menagerie of people. The sights and sounds transported me back to Granny Morgan's where my family would meet for weekly Sunday dinners. The dark oak floors of the dining room shone like polished glass. Off-white wainscoting complimented the flowered wallpaper. Country blue molding and chair rails tied everything together like a photo in *Southern Living* magazine.

High ceilings, painted to match the wainscot, were accented with heavy oak beams and chandeliers that hung over each large family style table. The smell of frying chicken and freshly baked biscuits swirled around me like ghosts from a time gone by.

My eyes scanned the room, and I observed guests partaking of homemade dishes. Others sat with heads close together, talking and laughing, all of them oblivious to our troubles.

Nana interrupted my thoughts. "Why, there's Joyce, and that nice, young nephew of hers. He had the cot set up in our room in no time at all. They just don't make 'em like that anymore. Except for Beau, of course," she added, with a sharp elbow to my ribs.

Joyce approached and led us to a large round table already occupied by Sheriff Wheeler. "Ladies, I hope you enjoy your meal. If you need anything, be sure and let me know." She gave us a smile and went off to tend to other guests.

"Good evening." Sherriff Wheeler greeted us by standing up,

offering out a chair to Nana and when she'd accepted, pushed it in with a chivalrous flare.

I gaped after Joyce, now chatting at another table. Why did she seat us here? She had to have made a mistake.

Nana floated out her napkin.

"Nana, get up. We're going to find another table." I placed a hand on her chair back.

"Trixie, what's gotten into you? There's nothing wrong with this table, and I'm not moving." She stuck to the seat like glue. She made goo-goo eyes at the sheriff. Not long ago, I thought he was easy on the eyes. Things change. Right this minute he didn't look so good to me. His sidekick, Deputy Ray, plodded across the room and, with a nod, sat next to him.

"Trixie, sit down. You're making a scene," Dee Dee pleaded. Her face paled in the dim light.

How dare he do this to her! Couldn't he leave us alone long enough to eat in peace? I had a gut feeling this was a set up.

"Trixie, why don't you introduce your young friend? I don't believe we've met." The sheriff met my eyes.

Oh puleeeeeeeese.

Nana grinned from ear to ear.

"Sheriff Wheeler, this is my great-aunt. Nana, this is Sheriff Wheeler." I reluctantly sat down, and settled my napkin. "Shouldn't you be out looking for John Tatum's murderer?"

He met my gaze with equal measure, and then turned back to my aunt. "It's a pleasure to make your acquaintance, Ma'am. I see where your niece gets her good looks." He shook Nana's hand and held it longer than necessary.

The waiters brought large bowls of mashed potatoes, green beans, potato salad, and baked beans and sat them on the table. Silence ensued for the next few minutes while everyone filled their plates. I needed energy, so I wasn't going to let this put a damper on my appetite. Looking at the mountains of mashed potatoes piled on the other plates, I could tell no one else was, either.

After several minutes, the sheriff disclosed the reason for this sup-posedly impromptu meeting. "I heard you've been asking some ques-tions of our local citizens."

"That's what writers do, Sheriff Wheeler." I gave him a sickeningly sweet smile.

"You know what I mean. This is serious, and I'm not going to be responsible for what might happen to you." The sheriff put both hands on the edge of the table and gave me his now famous "I'm not kidding" look.

"All right, I won't hold you responsible." I had no intention of giving in yet. I had leads to follow. I returned his look with my best "I'm not giving up" stare.

He continued. "I have some information that might lead us to another suspect. This could possibly clear Dee Dee once and for all. It's being checked into as we speak." He leaned in further towards me, returned my gaze, and didn't look away.

What beautiful blue eyes you have, Jake.

"I promise to let you know if anything transpires from the lead. Now, you promise to leave the investigation to us."

He looked so satisfied; I hated to burst his bubble. "That's great news Sheriff, but I'm not sure I can do that. I have more people to interview for my article. I can't help it if they're acquaintances of Tatum's. It's a small town, after all."

His demeanor changed in a millisecond. He grumbled, just loud enough for me to hear. "Look, Ms. Montgomery, I've tried being nice to you. I know this has been hard on you and Ms. Lamont, but stay out of where you don't belong. Consider yourself warned." With hands on the edge of the table, he pushed his chair back and nodded to Deputy Ray.

"But, I'm not through eating yet." The deputy met his boss's eyes and he changed his mind. "Oh. I guess I've had enough." He scooted his chair back and tipped his hat to us. "Ladies."

With that, we watched the local law enforcement, and any olive branch they might have offered, storm out of the restaurant.

CHAPTER TWENTY

The rest of our meal subdued, we finished our dessert and retreated to our room.

"Trixie, you heard what that handsome sheriff said. Are you going to mind him?" Only Nana had the nerve to ask, but I saw the same question mirrored on Dee Dee's face.

"Nana, I really *am* working on an article. Remember, that's why I came to Dahlonega in the first place. I'm just taking the opportunity to ask questions that might help Dee Dee while I'm at it. What if I trust the sheriff, who wants to run for mayor, and he slams the case closed? And Dee Dee behind bars!"

"Put that way, it's as clear as the nose on my face. That's why you need my help." She had a glint in her eye that scared me. I half-expected her to grab her jacket and pocketbook again and head out the door. "Together, I bet we can not only clear Dee Dee, but solve who did this terrible thing."

"Uh, that's great Nana. I'm sure you'll be an asset." It was late; I didn't have the energy to argue. I still had research to do before I could go to sleep. I looked to the closed door and sighed. "Dee Dee's sure been in the bathroom a long time."

"That girl needs to see a doctor. It's like watching a commercial with the leaky pipe people!"

Right then, the door flew open, and in Dee Dee bounced, dressed in her bright green kitty pajamas.

"Well, who let the cats out?" Nana asked. I doubled over in a fit of laughter.

"Very funny," she said as she grinned. "Y'all are jealous because you don't have any p.j.s like this." She modeled for us, to our hoots of laughter.

"You're right." We both laughed and applauded.

Dee Dee gingerly made her way to the roll away bed and straightened out the blankets. She sat down and sighed.

"How are you really doing, Dee Dee?" I clasped her hand and pressed my lips together in a smile. I wanted to help her so badly. I couldn't imagine being in her shoes.

"I feel a little better since Sheriff Wheeler told us he has another person of interest. Isn't that good news?" She shook off her matching kitty slippers and put her feet on the bed.

"Yes, it is. I won't be satisfied, though, until they've made an arrest. Then I'll breathe easy." I spoke slowly, watching Nana grab her toothbrush and jammies and head to the bathroom. I made sure the door closed tight before I lowered the boom.

"I plan on driving out to the Hawkins' in the morning. From everything we've been told, Tommy could be a prime suspect. I'm not sure what reason I'm going to use for an interview. I don't suppose I could tell him I'm doing a story about stills, and someone told me he might have one in working condition?" I emitted a nervous laugh.

Dee Dee smiled, but shook her head. "Very funny, but I don't think so. Approaching the Hawkins clan sounds dangerous to me." She pulled the covers up to her nose.

"I'll come up with some idea tomorrow. I have to."

"Well, if you insist on going, I'm going with you. After all, you're doing this for me. The least I can do is help." Dee Dee wore the look she would don when she was dead set on doing something. I didn't even try to talk her out of it. My problem was to figure out how to keep Nana from joining us.

Dee Dee smoothed the bed covers. "I called Sarah to see how things were at the shop. She told me not to worry, business couldn't be better.

And she was fine working alone. I hope when I reach her age I can be as active as she is."

We sat and discussed what we had learned from talking with Miranda and Sueleigh. Both of us were in a lighter mood with the news that Sheriff Wheeler had another person of interest. In a few minutes, Nana emerged from the bathroom wearing a nightie that had surely been ordered from Victoria's Secret.

Something was definitely going on with Nana. What would cause this gray-haired little lady to become so flirtatious lately? I had many memories of my spunky great-aunt, but flirting shamelessly was not one of them. Now the sexy nightie? I would have to keep a watch on her.

Even though it wasn't quite dark, Nana and Dee Dee had settled down to sleep. I turned off the big light and used my book light to read from one of the Dahlonega research books I'd brought from home.

Harv had asked me to look for a murder that took place during the original gold rush days and, after looking at several books, I found an unsolved murder I thought would make a good article.

In the early 1930s, a farmer named Donnie Haygood lived and worked the land that had been handed down through generations of his family. His great-grandfather, Micah Haygood, had won the acreage in the Cherokee Land Lottery. Micah hoped to find gold, but was unsuccessful. The spread became a working farm, and the Haygoods spent their spare time looking for gold.

Tired of working his farm, Donnie decided to sell and move into town, hoping to offer his children a better life. He promised the property to a buyer, but before the transaction took place, Donnie discovered gold and backed out of the deal.

A few days later he was found dead behind the assayer's office.

I screwed my lips and tried to remember if I'd seen or heard anything about this at the gold museum. I yawned and set the light and the book down, unable to keep my eyes open any longer.

It seemed I'd just laid down when my eyes opened to light peeping through the curtains. Propped up on one elbow, I craned my neck to see the alarm clock. The lighted face of the clock showed it was nearly seven. I seriously considered turning over and going back to sleep. In my dazed, half-awake, half-asleep state, my dream of a handsome cowboy tempted me to resume snoozing.

But sleeping in was not a luxury I could afford. Important interviews waited. I wanted to interview Tommy Hawkins as soon as possible. I willed myself to jump up and rush around with enthusiasm, but I couldn't. *Cowgirl up!* It took several minutes before I could force my tired body from the bed.

It wasn't easy maneuvering around Dee Dee's cot. I stumbled, bumped into her bed, and fell over on a wadded up body.

"What the ...." Dee Dee shot up like a jack-in-the-box.

I held my sore knee. "I'm sorry, Dee Dee."

"Are you okay?" She asked with concern in her voice, and rubbed sleep from her eyes.

"Yeah, I'm all right." I held my painful knee. "I hit my knee. I tried to be quiet."

"Need me to do anything?" She spoke in a sleep-slurred voice.

"No. Go back to sleep. I'm going to get a shower. We've got a lot to accomplish today."

She rolled over, covered up, and started snoring.

Another head popped up on the other bed, reminding me of a bobble-head doll. "What's going on over there?"

Nana! "Nothing, Nana, everything's fine. You can go back to sleep."

She did, and right quick, two of my favorite people in the world snored in unison.

When I flipped on the bathroom light, a big black spider fled the scene. I looked around for any other creepy, crawly creatures sharing quarters with the spider. Coast clear! I turned on the water as warm as I could stand it.

Several minutes of warm water relaxed my tight muscles. I toweled off and dressed as quietly as possible. I applied a double dose of makeup to cover the dark bags that had sprung up, literally overnight.

I would need all the help I could get this day if I were to charm a story out of the likes of the Hawkins clan!

CHAPTER TWENTY-ONE

When I exited the bathroom, I noticed Dee Dee rummaging in her suitcase for something to wear.

"Oh, you're up."

"Of course I'm up. Who could sleep when someone careens into her bed with the force of a tidal wave?"

She must have seen the look of surprise on my face, grinned, and said, "Just kidding! I thought I'd lighten the mood a little."

"I wouldn't try to lighten the mood too often. I'm on my last nerve, and it's frayed." With my nervous energy, I was pretty sure I could hand-power a light bulb.

I changed the subject to safer ground. "What do you think about a light breakfast so we can get an early start?"

"That sounds good." Dee Dee leaned over and whispered "What about Nana? Is she going with us?"

"No way! I've been bouncing around ideas. I'm sending her on an important mission. It should keep her busy until we get back."

"What are you girls talking about?" Nana piped up.

"I told Dee Dee I need your help this morning. I have an important errand for you to run while Dee Dee and I go interview someone for my article."

She sat up. "Sure, doll. I'll do anything I can to help. Remember, that's why I'm here." She grinned from ear to ear. "What do you need me to do?"

Dee Dee made her way to the bathroom while Nana and I continued our conversation. "I took some pictures to go along with my article, and they need to be printed right away. Harv wants to see them as soon as possible. Do you think you can find a store that will print them in an hour or two? Just check out the merchants on the square; I don't want you going any further."

If all went as planned, getting the pictures printed should keep Nana busy and out of trouble until we returned.

"Well, yes. I can do that. But why can't I go with you and Dee Dee?" she pouted. "I can take care of the pictures when we get back."

Shoot, this wasn't going as easy as I'd hoped. *Think quick Trixie.*

"It might be noon by the time we get back. There's a corner drugstore that opens at ten. Ask the clerk if she can put them on a computer disc as well as print them, and then I can send them to Harv as soon as I get back. I really need your help with this." I said a quick prayer for her compliancy. Harv didn't need the pictures right away, but I needed to keep Nana busy and safe.

"I guess you're right dear. That Harv sure can be a nasty person, though. You'd think a burr was stuck up under his saddle the way he grumbles all the time."

I couldn't help laughing. Anyone who didn't know Harv personally could easily come to that conclusion.

Minutes later we walked out the door. Dee Dee and I had dressed in jeans and long sleeve shirts and Nana had on another of her jogging ensembles. You could call us the three Musketeers.

Someone had laid out a continental breakfast of pastries and coffee in the lobby for those who didn't want to eat in the dining room. We chatted with Joyce while we ate sticky buns and drank steaming hot coffee. I filled her in on our plan to visit the Hawkins' place.

"You'd better watch your backs if you are determined to go out there," she warned. "By the way, did you get a chance to talk with Miranda yesterday?

"Uh, yes. I talked with her." I wondered why Joyce wanted to know, if she was just nosey, or if she had another reason for asking.

"Do you think she had anything to do with Tatum's murder?" She took another sip of coffee. "I wouldn't be surprised, the way she ranted and raved about his infidelity."

"Well..." I took a breath, weighing whether or not to divulge Miranda and my conversation.

"If you ask me, he got what he deserved." Joyce's nostrils flared with distaste in a way that seemed out of character for the nice innkeeper.

"Why would you say that?" I leaned forward.

"J-just imagine how furious he made somebody, in order to be murdered in such a violent way. With a pickaxe!"

"Yes. Imagine." I blinked down at the remainder of my now unappetizing bear claw. Whether or not it was true, I still thought it an odd thing for her to say.

Dee Dee and I finished our coffee, and left Nana talking to Joyce and Leroy, "that nice young nephew of hers" who creeped the heck out of me.

We stepped outside, a little nip in the air greeting us. A slight breeze blew as gentle as an angel's breath. It was the beginning of another beautiful day. Only a few vendors had ventured out this early in the morning. Others walked up the steps of the local parish, the steeple bell ringing out a Sunday morning welcome.

"I feel guilty we're not going to church." Dee Dee sniffed. "Especially with everything that's going on."

"Let's pray, quick." I took her hands in mine, knowing we needed our Father's direction.

Dee Dee prayed. "Heavenly Father, please keep us safe and help us to find John Tatum's real killer... In Jesus' name. Amen."

I contributed a hearty, "Amen!" and felt stronger for it.

I followed the haphazard directions Sueleigh gave us. From the rear-view mirror, I saw the town fade away. The golden leaves of the surrounding forest glowed in the morning sunlight. The twists and turns of the mountainous road dictated the speed I drove. Leaves still clung to many of the trees, but along the side of the road, boulders were dusted in already fallen foliage. I was lost in my thoughts when Dee Dee spoke.

"This view takes my breath away," she said with a contented sigh.

"Mine, too. Doesn't it look like God created a kaleidoscope?"

"It sure does." After a minute of contemplation she spoke again. "Trix, I'm still concerned we're traveling so far out. What if something happens? You heard how mean Joyce said Tommy Hawkins is."

"I bet he's not that mean. She's probably exaggerating."

Like you believe that, Trixie. I shifted in my seat and peered at the twisting road all the more intently.

"Have you thought of any reasons I can give Tommy to interview him?" I thought about the moonshine still Hawkins hid in the woods. A story about the back woods would definitely earn brownie points from Harv.

"Since you're writing on the gold rush, why don't you use that as an opener? Most folks with roots from around here have someone in their families that mined gold."

"That could work. Thanks." As we drove, we talked about the kids, the cats, and anything else that kept us from dwelling on the inevitable meeting.

As we rounded a tight curve, I spied something furry skittering across the road at the double yellow line.

Dee Dee screamed, pointing ahead, "Watch out!"

CHAPTER TWENTY-TWO

I slammed on my brakes, the tires squealing. Both of us shot forward in our seat belts, the car now at a dead stop in the middle of the road. A quick check to the rear view showed no one was behind us. Thank goodness!

"Holy cow, what are you trying to do? Get us killed?" I clutched my heart. I pulled over to the side of the road to catch my breath. My knee screamed in agony.

"I'm sorry, Trix. I was afraid you didn't see the cat in the road."

"Well, I did see it, and I didn't plan on running it down. Anyway, what's a kitty doing in the road out in the middle of nowhere?"

Her eyebrows cocked and she shrugged her shoulders. "I suppose he was trying to get to the other side?"

The tension broke and, despite my throbbing knee, I joined Dee Dee in laughter stemming from hysteria. If this kept up, the stress from the past couple of days was bound to award us a very long vacation in the home for the bewildered.

Wiping tears from my eyes, I pulled back onto the highway and continued towards our destination. A couple of miles down the road we passed the sign for Amicolola Falls.

I asked Dee Dee to read me the directions to the Hawkins. Ten minutes later, we pulled onto a long dirt road, leading us to Tommy's house. As we made the turn, a bevy of butterflies played havoc in my stomach. What had I been thinking?

The scene before me could only be described as *Dukes of Hazzard* meets *Deliverance*. A faded reddish-orange Dodge Charger, with the number one on its side, and a rebel flag painted on top, was parked in the dirt yard. It was an exact replica of "General Lee." I looked around to see if Bo, Luke, and cousin Daisy stood nearby.

A wooden framed house, in need of a paint job, sat in a dirt yard that obviously required no maintenance. Someone had thought to spruce it up with a few leggy gold and yellow chrysanthemums stuck in an old washtub.

Several old hound dogs lay in the yard, under the porch, and on the porch. One yawned and scratched behind its ear. I counted five, no, six of them as we neared. None of them proved to be guard dogs, as they let us approach without barking. That was left up to the furious barks of the two Dobermans, chained mid yard, that produced enough noise to wake the dead.

My legs began to itch. I reminded myself to check for fleas later. Some of the other dogs barely lifted their heads, making a half-hearted effort to see the trespassers. None of them seemed too interested in us.

We exited the car, staying well out of the snarling dogs' reach, and precariously made our way toward the porch where a bear of a man now stood by the front door.

"I don't have a good feeling about this," Dee Dee whispered, her expression calm, but her voice at near-panic. "I think we should get back in the car and be on our way."

I agreed, but I wasn't giving up that quick.

"Don't worry, I can handle it." *Famous last words.*

"What are y'all doing on my property?" Backwoods Bob bellowed.

Obviously, Dee Dee didn't believe me when I told her I had it under control. "Uh, we made a wrong turn, and we're lost. Sorry we bothered you; we'll be on our way." She turned around and headed to the car.

I grabbed her by the shirt and jerked her back. It was her hide I was trying to save, and I wasn't going to do it alone. "Let me do the talking."

"Well, you go right ahead," She hissed. "But if he kills both of us don't complain to me."

"Are you Tommy Hawkins?" I asked with more bravado than I possessed.

"Yeah. What's it to ya?"

My mind went completely blank. "Dee, what was that reason we were going to give him for showing up unannounced?" I hissed out of the side of my lop-sided grin.

"Did you kill John Tatum?" Dee Dee hollered before I could get any words out.

So much for being subtle.

"Oops," Dee Dee clapped a shaking hand over her mouth.

"What'd you say?" Tommy shot in a nasally mountain drawl.

"Uh," I stammered. "Do you know who killed John Tatum?" I tried for a quick recovery.

"Naw, I don't. Whad I care anyways? Somebody beat me to it, that's all." He scratched his belly, like a dog begging for a good flea dip. "Who are you and why do ya want to know?"

"My name is Trixie Montgomery, and this is my assistant Dee Dee Lamont." If I kept referring to her as my assistant, Dee Dee was going to demand a paycheck pretty soon. "I'm a writer, working on a story."

"So what's that got to do with me or Tatum?" He scratched in a place that wasn't very gentlemanly.

This wasn't getting us anywhere. Dee Dee shuffle closer to the porch, and the Dobermans went wild. She stepped back, hands up in surrender. "Look, Mr. Hawkins; the truth is, I've been questioned about John Tatum's murder. I didn't do it, and we're trying to find out who did. The story around town is that you've had it in for Tatum ever since he shot and killed your brother, Tubby. Were you in town Friday evening?"

I took a deep intake of breath, "Are you nuts, Dee Dee?" Backwoods Bob spoke through the doorway, "Martha, get my gun!"

In an instant, the ugliest woman I've ever laid eyes on appeared in the doorway. She stood at least six feet tall, and was built like a University of Georgia linebacker. The maroon hair was no doubt a dye job gone wrong. Overalls completed the package.

Martha must have been standing right by the door, for she instantly handed Tommy a shotgun. Dee Dee went running, and I limped towards the car. Shots rang out. We slammed the doors as fast as we could. I turned the ignition. Nothing!

"Start the car, Trixie!" Dee Dee yelled.

"What do you think I'm trying to do? It won't start," I shouted right back.

I jumped when the phone rang. "Grab that," I yelled.

"Harv, it's me Dee Dee! We're being shot at. Trixie can't get her car to start. She'll call you later." I could hear Harv's voice coming through the phone. Dee Dee disconnected. "My, he sure has a colorful vocabulary."

Oh, boy. Harv was going to be upset about this. But right now, his anger paled in comparison to gunshots.

I continued to turn the key with such force it was a wonder it didn't break. Still nothing!

Suddenly, Dee Dee shrieked.

I looked over at her, face corpse-white. She pointed a finger, and I hazarded a glimpse out my window, fully expecting the barrel of Tommy Hawkins' shotgun to be the last thing I ever saw.

CHAPTER TWENTY-THREE

Instead of double barrels, Sheriff Wheeler stood, nose to glass, outside my driver's side window. "Sheriff Wheeler!" I sputtered, and rolled it down.

"Oh my goodness, are we glad to see you! That man tried to kill us!"

I couldn't believe he was laughing. "If he'd wanted to kill you, Trixie, he wouldn't have shot over your head." He turned toward the porch and the pack of dogs. "Tommy, put that gun down. Now! I don't want to have to run you in."

"Aw, Sheriff, I warn't going to hurt 'em. Them two were askin' me questions about Tatum's killin'. Then they started askin' me 'bout Tubby's death. It ain't none of their business."

"I'll take care of them. You go on back in the house," the sheriff ordered. Stretched to his tallest height, he stood in a pose that meant business. He made a formidable sight.

Tommy scratched his protruding stomach. Much to my relief, he turned and went in the house. Martha followed.

Sheriff Wheeler leaned down and stuck his head in the window. He was so close, I could see his eyelashes.

"Hello, Dee Dee." He backed up and looked me in the eyes. He wasn't laughing anymore. "I suppose this was your idea to come out here and question Tommy?" Before I could answer, he started lecturing me.

"I thought I told you to keep your nose out of where it doesn't belong. You could have gotten hurt. You might not care about yourself, but you could have been responsible for putting your friend in danger."

"Well, since you put it that way—"

"You're lucky I was here to help. It might have turned out a lot worse."

I quickly made a decision to forego my guilt for the time being. "Well, it turned out all right."

"Because I showed up," he cautioned. "What were you going to do if you couldn't start your car?"

I didn't want to say that I would have probably called 9-1-1. "How did you know we were here, anyway?"

"I went by the Dahlonega Inn to find you. Joyce told me you came out here. I had a feeling you might be in trouble. Tommy Hawkins doesn't take kindly to strangers. Heck," he pushed his hat up on his head. "Tommy doesn't take kindly to anybody."

Dee Dee leaned towards the window. "Well, I for one am glad to see you. That maniac was trying to kill us. When Trixie's car wouldn't start, I pictured us shot full of holes."

"Traitor," I muttered under my breath, then turned back to my reluctant hero. "Well, Sheriff, why were you looking for us?"

"Let's get your car started first so we can go back and talk in my office." He raised the hood on my archaic Jeep. I'm not sure what he did, but in the shake of a sheep's tail, she was purring like a kitten. I looked up to the heavens and whispered, *Thank you*, then stuck my head out of the window to peer where he slammed the hood. "How did you do that?"

He sauntered back and placed his hands on the doorframe of the open window. "Well, Ms. Montgomery, if you'd clean off the battery cables once in a while, you'd stand a much better chance of it starting when you get yourself in trouble."

If I didn't consider myself a lady I'd have smacked that devilish grin right off his face. Then again, maybe not. I wouldn't want to mar that gorgeous mug. I rolled up the window, defining a clear barrier between us.

I was still shaking as we followed him the long drive back to town. Dee Dee sat beside me, arms crossed, muttering how I almost got her killed and how she was now about to be arrested. I felt a wee bit guilty that I hadn't heeded everyone's warnings, but I had Dee Dee's welfare in mind. "Don't be so sure; if he were going to arrest you, he would have done it on the spot."

"Then why not just tell us whatever he had to say."

"I don't know, but I'm glad to be putting distance between us and the Hawkins."

We arrived at the station and Dee Dee asked first thing, "Where's the bathroom?"

I wasn't surprised. I had to admit, after our harrowing morning, I needed a potty break, too.

After necessaries were taken care of, an officer escorted us to Jake's office. The dilapidated chairs were obviously used for interrogating prisoners. When I plopped down, it was as hard as frozen ground. The stuffing had flattened out in all the strategic places. No matter how I adjusted my bottom, I couldn't get comfortable.

Pictures of past sheriffs, dating back to the late 1800's, covered the walls. The décor could have been called Early American Male. No bright or cheerful colors enlivened the room. The furniture, including the desk, was purely for functional purposes. Aesthetics had not been taken into consideration during the decorating.

Sheriff Wheeler's desktop was covered in papers, making it impossible to see what it looked like. Either he was a busy man with a lot of work, or a man who did little work. The bright sun through dusty blinds illuminated him from behind. He leaned back in his desk chair and clasped his hands behind his head.

"I told you I'd find out who killed Tatum if it wasn't Dee Dee." He grinned from ear to ear.

Did this mean what I thought it meant?

"Who was it?"

"Was it Miranda Tatum or Sueleigh Dalton?" Dee Dee and I asked questions in unison, both of us on the edge of our seats with excitement.

"What makes you think it was either one of them?" Sheriff Wheeler asked.

"They both had a motive. A woman scorned makes for one angry woman."

He stared at me intently. "Are you speaking from experience, Trixie?"

Ouch. I glared back at him. "I don't see what that has to do with this, Sheriff. Are you going to tell us who it is?"

CHAPTER TWENTY-FOUR

Y ou're wrong on both accounts. "It was neither Miranda Tatum, nor Sueleigh Dalton. Nor Dee Dee."

"What?" I exclaimed.

"You heard me right, Trixie."

I was so happy. I would be glad to extend my gratitude to anyone who solved the case. If that was Sheriff Wheeler, then so be it.

"Thank you Sheriff. Does this mean Dee Dee is free to go?"

I looked at Dee Dee. She stared straight ahead, her eyes blank. Then a great big smile covered her face. It must have registered—she was free!

"Who did it?" I asked. "And why did they do it?"

"I can't tell you who it is at this point, but it appears that someone was blackmailing Tatum. We found a large amount of cash in John's pocket and more on the floor. The museum was their meeting place for the cash exchange. Something went wrong this time, and the perpetrator lost it. This person grabbed the pickaxe and used it as a weapon to kill John. And, we have a confession."

"We told you all along Dee Dee didn't kill him," I said with great satisfaction.

"Since Dee Dee was found holding the murder weapon, we had to consider her a person of interest. When we found a large amount of cash on Tatum, we wondered if there was more to this murder than first met the eye. We pursued some tips and hit the jackpot."

When Dee Dee spoke I could barely hear her. "I can't believe it's over." She began to cry as she reached and grabbed my hand. Tears pooled in my eyes, too.

"You can believe it, Dee Dee. You're free to go. On the way out, please leave your addresses with the officer at the front desk. We might need you to come back and testify at the trial." He stood up, indicating the meeting was over.

"Thank you, Sheriff." The words almost stuck in my throat, but I hoped I looked sincere, anyway.

"One more thing." He ran his fingers through his hair. "I want you to lay off the sleuthing before you get someone killed."

"Sure thing," I said. I was so grateful we didn't need to.

We thanked him, and high-tailed it out of his office. As soon as we got out the front door, we hugged each other and let the tears flow.

"Come on, Dee Dee. Let's go tell Nana. I'm so glad this is over. I'm going to call Beau as soon as we get back to the Inn. He saw something in Sheriff Wheeler we didn't see. I didn't think he was trying very hard to find the right person. This is one time I don't mind being wrong." I hooked my arm through Dee Dee's and lead her towards the car.

"I've been so scared. I knew I was innocent, but it's kinda hard to prove when you're found standing over the body with the murder weapon in your hands. I'm so grateful for all your help. I have no doubt, Sheriff Wheeler wouldn't have looked further than his nose to find Tatum's killer if you hadn't insisted he look elsewhere. I can't wait to thank Beau, too. He's such a sweetheart."

Yes he is, I thought.

It was afternoon, and the streets were crowded with people enjoying the festivities. I had an urge to shout at them to stop and join in our celebration.

With a silent thanks to Sheriff Wheeler, I was relieved when the car started right up this time. We traveled at a snail's pace as we precariously made our way through the throng of tourists. We pulled into the parking lot and walked to our room.

"What's going on with you two?" Nana asked as we entered through the door, our grins a dead giveaway. "Good grief, you two look like a couple of raccoons! Where have you girls been?" She handed me an envelope. I assumed the pictures were inside. "Go ahead and open it up."

I did. It was full of pictures, as well as a CD, exactly as I'd asked. "Good job, Nana." I leaned down and gave her a kiss on the cheek. "Nana, we've got great news to tell you. Go ahead, Dee Dee. Tell her."

"You're not going to believe this. I've been completely exonerated. They've found out who killed John Tatum." She gave Nana a big bear hug, and Nana hugged her back. She stepped back and did a little jig. "I'm free, I'm free!"

While we danced around and acted like we didn't have any good sense, someone knocked on the door. I opened it to see a distraught Sueleigh Dalton standing in the doorway. Her blouse was unevenly buttoned, and her hair stood askew. She was crying. "You've got to help me, Trixie. You've just got to help me."

"Sueleigh, what's the matter?"

"Don't just let her stand there. Ask her in," Nana quipped.

"Uh, sure. Come on in, Sueleigh." I grabbed her by the arm and pulled her into the room.

"I'll get you some tissues." Dee Dee headed to the bathroom.

I had visions of Dee Dee holing up in the bathroom in order to escape the inevitable. She wasn't getting off that easy. "That's a great idea Dee Dee, but don't get lost," I called as she hurried off. My attention turned to the distraught young woman.

Nana led her to one of the beds and wrapped a grandmotherly arm around her. "There now, dear. Dry up those tears. We can't understand a word you're saying through all that hiccupping."

Dee Dee reappeared. Sueleigh took the tissues and blew her nose, honking like a sick penguin. I didn't realize an attractive young woman could make such a disgusting sound.

Dee Dee and I sat on the bed across from them.

Nana gave Sueleigh a minute to wipe her nose and dry her eyes, then launched in. "All right, young lady. What is it that you think Trixie can help you with?"

"They arrested Daddy. They said he killed John," she managed to get out between sobs. "I know he didn't do it. You'll help me prove it, won't you?"

CHAPTER TWENTY-FIVE

What makes you think I can help?"

She sniffed and snorted before answering. "You helped your friend, and I thought you might help me, too. You seem like such a nice lady."

I wanted to help, but I had a deadline to meet.

"Sheriff Wheeler told us someone gave a confession. I didn't know it was your father. I don't know what I can do to help."

"He confessed to blackmailing John. He never confessed to murdering him," she said.

I couldn't believe this was happening. My head spun, and I struggled to breathe. The room was out of focus. A minute ago we were celebrating; now it felt like the air had been let out of my balloon. I imagined Dee Dee wasn't feeling much better because she grabbed my arm and gave it a death squeeze.

Thoughts swirled around in my mind. If Frank Dalton didn't kill Tatum, who did? Would the focus turn back to Dee Dee? I had been riding an emotional roller coaster since this had begun. I didn't know how much more I could stand.

"Sueleigh, what makes you think he didn't kill John?" It was a practical question, so I couldn't understand why she looked at me like I'd gone around the bend.

"Because he told me he didn't," she sputtered with indignation.

"I realize he's your father, Sueleigh, and you love him dearly. Of course, you want to believe him. Just because he said he didn't kill Tatum doesn't mean he didn't do it."

"That's right," chimed in Dee Dee. I dared to glance over at her. All the happiness I'd seen a few minutes ago had vanished and had been replaced by eyes as wide as saucers.

"Let's all calm down. Sueleigh, start from the beginning. What did you mean when you said your daddy confess he had blackmailed this man?"

"It's like I told you. He was blackmailing John. As soon as I found out they had arrested Daddy, I went straight to the jail. He told me all about it." She had calmed down enough to talk without gulping for air.

"What did he tell you?" I asked, attempting to be as encouraging as possible.

"I know it wasn't right that he blackmailed John, but I don't blame him. After the way John blew me and the baby off, it's no wonder Daddy found a way to get back at him."

I agreed he had a reason, but that didn't make it right.

She blew her nose and proceeded with her story. "Daddy said he was just getting John to pay us what he owed. He's never paid one red cent in support for the baby. Daddy said it was his responsibility to pay and if I wouldn't make him, he would. I always thought he was just blowing off steam. But he did. He didn't feel guilty about it, either." She looked me straight in the face. "He may have been blackmailing him, but I know for a fact he didn't kill him."

"You've told us that before Sueleigh, but how do you know that for a fact?"

"Because he told me what happened." She stopped. I silently willed her to continue. "It's like this."

As we leaned closer, she studied the wadded tissues.

"A couple of months ago, Daddy was volunteering for the Community Charity Auction. He was helping sort through the donations. You should have seen some of the stuff. You couldn't give it away, much less sell it. Daddy found this box that was donated by the Tatums." She hesitated, drawing a deep breath.

"He went through the contents of the box to see if there was anything of value. He was so mad at John. I guess he figured there might be something he could sell on the side and give the money to me and the baby. He picked up an old family Bible, to move it out of the way, and something fell out of it."

"What?" we asked in unison.

"It was an envelope with instructions to be opened when old man Tatum died. It never was."

"Which old man Tatum? John's father?" I tried to put the pieces together.

"No, Joshua Tatum, John's grandfather. Daddy read the letter and found a deathbed confession by Joshua Tatum. Back in the thirties, a family named Haygood owned quite a bit of land during the gold rush days. Donnie Haygood had promised to sell the land to Joshua, but right before the deal went through, Donnie backed out."

Bang!

A sudden pounding at the door made us all jump.

"What now?" I got up to send whoever it was away.

I opened the door.

"Hi, Ms. Montgomery." Leroy pushed his head around the door so he could see who was in the room. "Just wondered how y'all are doing and if there's anything you need. Hi there, Sueleigh."

She gave him a little wave.

"We're doing just fine, Leroy. Thanks for asking. Now if you don't mind, we're kind of busy right now." I held the door firmly to keep him from coming in any further.

"Well, all right, but be sure and let me know if there's anything I can get y'all."

"We sure will." I pushed the door closed with a click and bolted the lock, and rolled my shoulders. That guy still gave me the willies.

CHAPTER TWENTY-SIX

I know the Haygood story. I read about it last night." I plopped down and bid Sueleigh continue.

She nodded. "Local mystery, you know. But, here's the part that no one knew. Donnie Haygood decided not to sell the land to ole' man Tatum. Tatum already knew that the land held gold when he offered to buy it. Donnie had discovered gold right before he signed the papers. That's when he decided to back out of the deal."

I wondered what connection this story had to John Tatum's murder, but kept quiet.

"This made ole' man Tatum madder than a wasp with an infected stinger. He wrote in the letter that he had killed Donnie. Can you believe it? John's grandfather a murderer."

We shook our heads back and forth.

"They never caught the murderer," I offered, remembering the story.

"Where did you read about this murder Trixie?" Dee Dee asked.

"I was researching old murder cases for an article. The Haygood case was one that I read about."

I crossed my arms, looking to Sueleigh. "This solves the murder of Donnie Haygood, but what about John?"

"After he killed Donnie, he bought the land from his widow. He acted like he was doing her a favor so she could move into town and get work. He admitted he gave her a pittance for her land, but nowhere near what it was worth. Shortly after the purchase, he 'discovered' gold on the property. The Tatum Empire was built with blood money. I'd have loved to see John's face when Daddy showed him that letter." Tears glinted in the corner of her eyes.

"Wow, unbelievable." Dee Dee said, the weight of the solved mystery obviously sinking in. "So when your daddy found the letter, he saw the chance to blackmail John?"

"Yes, and it worked. John was willing to pay any amount to keep the information under wraps. He didn't want anyone to know that his grandfather was a cold-blooded murderer. He didn't want anything to dirty the Tatum name. Not even an illegitimate daughter." The tears flowed down her cheeks.

"It still doesn't prove your daddy's innocence," I said. "If anything, this could be used against him."

"That's what the sheriff said. But Daddy said that was plum crazy. He was getting a lot of money from him, so why would he want to mess up the money flow? He'd been meeting John every Friday at the museum where he gave the money to Daddy. That day, John never showed up. When it got close to closing time, Daddy left."

My mind drifted back to the day I interviewed Teresa. Tourists roamed from room to room at the museum. I tried to remember if I'd seen Frank in the stream of faces.

"Daddy didn't kill John. I just know he didn't. Please, you've got to help me. Since you're already looking for the real killer you can clear Dee Dee and Daddy at the same time. Please!" She closed her hands together and placed them under her chin as if she were praying.

I looked to Dee Dee and Nana for help. Their response: silence.

"I'm not sure I'm the right person to ask, Sueleigh. I'm not quali-fied to help your father. You need a professional." That was not the only reason I hesitated; I swallowed my guilt feelings. No way would I clear Frank if it aimed the spotlight back on Dee Dee. We'd come too far and had tasted freedom.

"Why didn't your father tell the sheriff this story?" Nana asked.

"He did. Sheriff Wheeler said because Daddy used the letter to black-mail John, it made him look guilty. He called it incriminating evidence.

Daddy confessed to blackmailing John, but he never confessed to killing him." Her eyes still glistened with tears.

My esteem for the Sheriff went down another notch, and I was beginning to feel like I might cry any minute, too.

"Sheriff Wheeler must have built his hunky body by jumping to conclusions," I snorted, to a trio of their nervous laughter. "If he jumped to conclusions with Dee Dee, he could have jumped to conclusions with Sueleigh's father, as well."

Jump, jump, jump - brain fog clouded my mind, and I felt on the edge of hysteria at the hopeful look on her face.

"Look Sueleigh, why don't you get something to eat? It's way past lunchtime, and we'll all feel better if we have something to eat. I can think better on a full stomach."

"Are you going to help?" Sueleigh asked. Her face brightened with expectation.

"Let me see what I can do. I'll go over this with Dee Dee and see if we can come up with any ideas. In the meantime, ask your father if he can think of any evidence that might clear him. I'm afraid it doesn't look good."

Tears welled up again in her swollen eyes and poured down her mascara-streaked face. *Way to go, Trixie.*

I got up and walked Sueleigh to the door. "I'll try to think of something. Leave your number with me, and I'll contact you as soon as I have any new information." She handed me her business card: Sueleigh Dalton, Beauty Consultant for Creative Cosmetics. Why was I not surprised?

It was late afternoon by the time we went to eat lunch at one of the little sandwich shops. The crowd was thinning out. Most of the tourists had headed home, tomorrow a workday. The vendors were pulling up stakes and getting their materials together, moving slowly, weary and ready to close up shop.

"Trix." Dee Dee shook my arm, "Your turn to order!" I looked up at the waitress. She impatiently flicked her pencil against her pad, waiting on me. I didn't have much of an appetite, but I had to eat something.

"Give me the same thing she ordered," I said as I pointed to Dee Dee.

"Okey, dokey," the waitress said. "That'll be two corned beef with sauerkraut." She turned and hurried away.

I hate corned beef with sauerkraut. "Wait, Miss!" I shouted to get her attention.

She whirled around and put her hands on her hips.

"Just give me a chicken salad sandwich," I sheepishly shrugged, knowing my distraction was starting to get the better of me.

Between bites, we discussed Sueleigh's dilemma. Nana wanted to help her; Dee Dee was wary. I couldn't blame her. I'd be, too, if I were in her sneakers.

Would I hurt Dee Dee if I helped Frank Dalton? Could I possibly help both of them at the same time if another killer *was* on the loose? And if that were the case, would I be putting all three of us in danger?

CHAPTER TWENTY-SEVEN

Exhausted from a trying day, we turned in early. If the ghosts of the old miners could talk, they would have definitely been complaining about the three women who could out-snore a man any ole day.

I slept fitfully, my sleep haunted by dreams. Sometime during the night, I sat up, wide-awake. An idea popped into my mind like someone had opened my head and planted it there: I believed the murder of Donnie Haygood somehow tied in to the murder of John Tatum. I tossed and turned the rest of the night as I waited with anticipation for morning.

I thought it was still night when I heard Nana and Dee Dee talking. I sat up and rubbed the sleep from my eyes.

"Hey. Thought you'd never wake up," Dee Dee said.

Nana chimed in, "Good morning, Sleeping Beauty. I'm glad you've decided to join the world of the living."

"Good morning, Nana," I managed to reply between yawns.

"Where do we start digging?" Nana asked.

"Digging for what, Nana?" I asked in return.

"Don't play coy with me, Missy. You know what I'm talking about. Where do we begin to look for John's real killer so we can get poor Mr. Dalton out of jail?" Nana failed to mention that "poor Mr. Dalton" had gotten in jail by blackmailing Tatum.

"I'm still thinking. Why don't you and Dee Dee go and get us some doughnuts and coffee for breakfast? I'll get cleaned up while you're gone."

"Why don't we wait on you while you get ready?" Dee Dee asked. "Then we can all go together."

When Nana turned her back towards us I winked at Dee Dee, started rubbing my eye, and pointed at Nana.

"Trixie, have you got something in your eye? It looks like you can't keep it open," Dee Dee said.

"Yes, I think I do. Why don't you come in the bathroom and help me get it out?" We squeezed in the bathroom and I shut the door.

"Let me see," Dee Dee said. She was an inch from my face, pulling down my lower lid. "Hold still, if you want my help."

"I don't have anything in my eye except my eyeball. I was trying to get your attention," I hissed. "I need you to keep Nana busy this morning while I go over to the courthouse and look up some information. I have a hunch, but I don't want to say anything until I find out for sure."

Thirty minutes later, Dee Dee pushed Nana out the door to set out on their mission of taking more photographs.

I grabbed the phone and called Sueleigh to meet me at the courthouse. I dressed, threw on my sweater, grabbed my bag and hurried out the door.

The Gold Rush Days over, Dahlonega now resembled a ghost town. Hardly anyone wandered around the square. I took my car to the courthouse; it was just too far to walk with my aching knee.

I was in the deed room when Sueleigh finally arrived in a whirlwind of turned heads. A lone clerk stood behind the counter. Tables and chairs occupied the front of the room. Several people sat around the tables.

"Hi. I'm Trixie Montgomery and this is Sueleigh—"

"I know who she is. How can I help you?" The clerk's nostrils flared with distaste. In small towns, gossip spreads like weeds in a garden, and Dahlonega apparently was no different.

We acquired the material we needed and started the task of finding dirt on the real killer. Within an hour we hit pay dirt!

I made copies of the information and stuffed a stack of pages in my bag. Excitement welled within me and my heart raced at a fair clip. I couldn't wait to share my news back at the inn. Sueleigh and I were halfway down the courthouse steps when my phone rang.

"Trix, you've got to come as quick as possible. Something's wrong with Nana." Dee Dee sounded upset.

"What's wrong? Do I need to call 911?"

Sueleigh sidled up closer to hear the conversation.

"No! I mean, I don't think so. She, ah just got short-winded walking back to the room and wants you to come as soon as you can. She looks a little pale."

"I'm leaving now. I should be there in a few minutes." I punched the cell phone off and frowned.

I was worried about Nana, but something still didn't add up. Nana was fine this morning, and most of the time she had more energy than me and Dee Dee combined.

"Who's sick?" Sueleigh asked.

I filled her in.

"I have a friend who's an EMT. I can call him. It's the least I can do for you."

"I think we'll be okay," I said, although I wasn't sure. Something wasn't right. "Thank you though."

Her frown indicated she didn't believe me. I didn't believe me either, but I wasn't sure why. I thanked her for her help, and hurried back to the inn.

As I fumbled with the key, I listened for voices, but heard nothing. "Dee Dee? Nana?" I pushed the door open. A hand grabbed my arm and pulled me inside. The door shut behind me with a solid thud.

"Well, lookie who's here. Little Ms. Butt-in-sky."

I turned around to see who Leroy was talking about. Then it dawned on me. I was Little Ms. Butt-in-sky.

I heard Dee Dee's whimpering before I saw her. "I'm so sorry, Trix. He made me do it. He had a gun and said he'd shoot Nana if I didn't call you."

"And I take everything back I said about him being a nice, young man," Nana said, glaring daggers at Leroy. If they had been real, Leroy would have be a dead man. Nana and Dee Dee were sitting on one of the beds, their hands and feet bound by duct tape. Bad enough my best friend was trussed up like this, but an elderly woman?

"Nana, are you okay?"

"Of course I'm okay, but if I get my hands on that scallywag, he'll wish he'd never been born. I—"

Leroy pointed the gun at Nana. "Shut up, old woman. You're annoying me. I think you'll be the first to go."

My anger grew, lessening the affect of my fear. "Leroy, are you sure you want to do this?"

Duh, I guess he did, or he wouldn't be here, Trixie.

"You're dang right. It's your entire fault I had to take it this far."

"And why would that be?"

Dee Dee rolled her eyes. I knew what she was thinking: *Why can't Trixie ever keep her mouth shut?* She could be right. My mouth had gotten me in trouble more times than I wanted to remember.

"Sit!" He didn't have to tell me more than once. I went over and sat by Nana. I gave her arm a reassuring squeeze.

"Keep your hands to yourself," Leroy growled.

Nana stuck her tongue out at him.

"Why don't you just let us go?" I suggested. "It'll be a lot easier on you if you let us go now."

"No way. You know too much, and I ain't goin' to jail for murder."

"You?" Dee Dee asked. "You killed John Tatum?" The cat was out of the bag now. We were in deep. The best thing I could hope for was a confession from Leroy. If we got out of this alive, I imagined it would come in handy. If not, then maybe someone would find it. I snuck my hand into my sweater pocket.

"Did you, Leroy?" I spoke a little too loudly, but I didn't want him to hear me switch on the mini tape recorder.

CHAPTER TWENTY-EIGHT

I don't guess it'll hurt to tell you. You won't have a chance to pass it on." His sinister laugh sent a chill up my spine. "Yes, I killed him. I would've gotten away with it, too, if you hadn't stuck your big, fat nose where it didn't belong."

"Your friend was the perfect scapegoat." He emitted a spine-chilling laugh as he directed an evil glare in Dee Dee's direction. "She was dumb enough to pull out the pickaxe and get her fingerprints all over the murder weapon."

"Takes a dummy to know one," Nana pointed out.

I heard a deep intake of breath from Dee Dee. I didn't know if it was indignation from being called stupid or because of Nana's brassiness.

Leroy continued blabbing, ignoring Nana's comment. "The sheriff obliged me by making her the main suspect."

"Then you," he turned towards me as he continued. "You had to ask questions around town, playing Little Miss Private Investigator."

I sat a bit taller, though my heart was still pounded.

Leroy was on a roll. "I followed you to find out what you were up to. It paid off yesterday when I saw Sueleigh go into your room. I figured something was going on. When she came out I offered her a shoulder to cry on and us being the good friends we are, she spilled her guts. You couldn't leave well enough alone, could you?"

"Well..."

"Shut up." He shoved me and I fell back, striking my head hard enough against the wall to see stars.

"Hey, who do you think you're telling to shut up?" Nana put in her two cents worth.

"I'm telling you to shut up old lady."

Nobody tells Nana to shut up and gets away with it. Well, he definitely wouldn't have gotten away with it if he wasn't pointing a gun at her.

"Uh, just a minute, Leroy. What made you think we found out you killed Tatum?" I dared to ask, hoping he'd continue.

"I wasn't sure until this mornin'. My buddy over at the courthouse called and told me what you were up to. I'd come too far for you to mess up my plan. If you'd left things alone, your friend could've been free. Stupid females."

"What do you think I learned at the courthouse?" I hoped he didn't know everything. What I had found out could put all of us in danger, but if I were going to get a full confession and motive on tape, I needed to keep him talking.

"Why don't you tell me, Ms. Know-It-All?"

I figured I might as well. We had nothing to lose—except our lives. Before I could start, a knock at the door interrupted me. Thank God, somebody was going to save us. A rush of relief flowed through me.

"Leroy?"

Joyce! Thank heaven.

"Come on in." He ordered.

Joyce entered and looked around to take in the situation, but I could tell by the look on her face that she offered no salvation.

"Ms. Montgomery was just going to tell us what she found out at the courthouse this morning," Leroy sneered.

"Joyce! Why?" I blinked back tears, realizing now that she was just as deep in this as her nephew. "I hoped you weren't involved. Surely there's nothing worth taking someone's life for." The look she gave me should have turned me to stone.

"What do you know? Who are you to tell me what a life is worth? You think you know the whole story. You don't."

"I know your maiden name is Haygood, isn't it?" I was gambling with our lives by antagonizing her, but it was important to get her to admit her part. Out loud.

"Isn't that the man Sueleigh was telling us about?" Dee Dee asked. "How'd you figure that out?"

"I remembered seeing a certificate on the wall of Joyce's office when Leroy took me in to get change. The full name was Joyce Haygood Johnston." I studied Joyce's face.

"You're right Trixie, Haygood is my maiden name. The gold Joshua Tatum found on my grandparent's land should have been ours. After Grandpa died, Tatum coerced Grandmother into selling him the land and moving into town."

"That hardly seemed fair." I touched the recorder and hoped the batteries wouldn't die before she incriminated herself.

"He acted like he was doing her a favor." Joyce sniffed her distaste and continued. "She didn't have a choice. She had two children to support. After they moved off the land, he supposedly discovered gold. Daddy always said Grandmother believed Joshua Tatum killed my Grandpa so he could get the gold. She could never prove it, though. The Haygoods were considered nobodies. She would've never stood a chance against Joshua Tatum."

I looked over at Dee Dee and Nana. The way their mouths lay open, they could've easily been mistaken for Venus Fly Traps. I mirrored their thoughts, I'm sure. How could this nice, sweet lady be involved in something so sinister?

"Why seek revenge now, Joyce?" *Keep her talking.* "That was so long ago."

"Why, indeed," Joyce spat, words full of venom. "My family poured their sweat and blood into this inn. When Grandmother moved into town all those years ago, she began working at the inn as a maid. A maid! She labored like a slave for years so she could take care of her children.

"When we were old enough and had saved enough, my sister and I bought the inn. We wanted to take care of our family and pay them back for all their years of hard work. Of course, the Tatums owned the place." Her eyes narrowed and her face reddened. "We'd been making payments to the Tatums all these years so we could own it out right.

"We just about had it paid off, too, when she got cancer and died. Her insurance policy barely paid for the funeral expenses. It didn't begin to cover her medical expenses. Leroy and I have been trying our best to make ends meet so we could continue the payments. We were a couple behind and, according to the contract, John had the right to call in the loan if we missed any payments.

"We begged him to work with us. Oh no, not Mr. Fancy Pants. It wasn't enough that he'd bought up most of the town. He wanted the inn, too. He came to me, demanding that we pay the loan in full. Yeah," she snorted, "like that was going to happen. He knew it was an impossible task." She stopped to get her breath, and stared where my hand, holding the recorder, made my pocket bulge. Her brows lifted.

CHAPTER TWENTY-NINE

S he stepped closer, fists curling.

"Wait a minute," I blurted, and slipped my hand out nonchalantly. My mind whirled, thinking back to the image of Mr. Tatum on the day we arrived. "Is that what he was doing here Friday, when he came storming out of the lobby and ran into Dee Dee?"

"He was as angry as a raging bull," she nodded. "He told Leroy he wasn't going to wait any longer to start proceedings to call in the loan. Leroy and I talked it over, and decided we didn't have a choice. We had to move quickly if we wanted to keep the inn. We figured he deserved whatever he got. Leroy followed him over to the museum Friday afternoon. When he saw the chance, he took it."

"Stop talking. You've said too much." Leroy lifted the gun again.

Joyce actually looked contrite. "I really am sorry I had to involve you and Dee Dee. I liked you. But when a scapegoat fell right into our hands, we couldn't pass it up. Then you wouldn't leave well enough alone. How was I to know you would be as stubborn as a bulldog when it came to defending your friend? I sure never had any friends like that."

I was sorry she hadn't, but good grief, that wasn't any excuse for murdering someone. She let Leroy take another man's life and was going to let Dee Dee take the rap. To me, that came from the heart of someone very evil. Gooseflesh skittered over my arms, as if a shadow fell over the room.

*I will fear no evil...Thy rod and thy staff, they comfort me...*I prayed for guidance, for deliverance, for Dee Dee, for Nana, and even for poor, greedy Mr. Tatum.

"Yeah, and when the sheriff arrested Frank Dalton, you could have gotten Dee Dee off free and clear. But no, you had to play the part of a bleeding heart," Leroy waggled the gun at me. "Isn't that right, Aunt Joyce?"

"Isn't that right, Aunt Joyce?" Nana mimicked, breaking any spell that may have fallen over the hushed room. My goodness, was she trying to get us killed? I reached over and gave her arm a hearty squeeze in hopes of hushing her up.

"I said keep your hands to yourself," Leroy barked. "Aunt Joyce, what are we going to do with them? They know everything now."

I've heard you can never know too much. In this case, I definitely knew more than I wanted to. I couldn't imagine how we'd escape. "This is a fine mess you've gotten us into, Ollie," popped into my head, and I pressed in an insane laugh.

A banging at the door was an answer to our silent prayers. "EMTs! Open up! Someone called for the ambulance."

Leroy's focus shot from us, to the door, to Aunt Joyce. He motioned to her to take care of it, waving the gun off his target, and I saw my chance to make a move.

Thy rod and thy staff, they comfort me.

Fist curled around my cane, I crashed it down on his wrist as hard as I could. A sickening pop resounded on contact. The gun flew out of his grasp and it clattered to the floor.

"Aunt Joyce!" He hissed, hugging his broken wrist, and shoved me down with his other hand. "Send them away before they call the cops!"

Joyce moved in what seemed slow motion as my vision tunneled on that flash of silver laying on the floor. In the background, I could hear Nana and Dee Dee yelling toward the door for all they were worth.

"Help us!"

"We're kidnapped! Call the police!"

I looked from the weapon to Leroy, and held my gaze steady. One of us was going to pick it up and shoot the other. We stood, equally frozen, unmoving.

Lord, give me strength to save us. I prayed.

He flinched first in our game of Chicken. He knelt, reaching toward the gun, but I was closer. Before Leroy had a chance to get the weapon, I lunged between it and him.

When I came to, I was in a hospital bed with Dee Dee on one side and Nana on the other.

They twittered around me like mother hens protecting their chicks. I was sore all over and had a ferocious headache, but I was alive! I tried to move my leg, but pain seared my knee like a branding iron. I cried out in a hiss.

"Whoa there, Missy," Nana cooed. Her musical voice soothed my ears. "You've hurt your knee again, and the doc wants you to take it easy. I'll call the nurse and let her know you're awake and need some pain medicine."

I looked from Nana to Dee Dee. "What happened?" They started talking at the same time, and I waved at them to stop. "Hold up; I can't understand what you're saying."

"Dee Dee, you tell her," Nana acquiesced.

"Oh, Trix. I'm so glad you're all right." Dee Dee stood grinning like the cat who ate the cream. "I never figured you for the hero type, but you've sure proved me wrong. Do you remember getting the gun from Leroy?"

"The last thing I remember is taking a nose dive to the floor so he wouldn't get it after I knocked it out of his hand."

"You mean broke his hand! You should have seen yourself, flying through the air. You moved quicker than an alley cat chased by a dog. You and Leroy got there the same time and you butted heads. I thought for sure you'd have a skull fracture. Knocked you both right out."

"The EMTs?" I asked, wondering about the knock at the door that saved us.

"Sueleigh asked one of her EMT friends to come and offer us a hand. She was worried about you. When they heard the ruckus, they broke the door in.

"I thought Joyce was going to have a heart attack right then and there. And if that wasn't enough excitement, Sheriff Wheeler saw the ambulance heading towards the inn and followed them. He and Deputy Ray showed up the same time they did."

"Nana and I told them what happened, and he arrested Joyce and Leroy right on the spot. Put handcuffs on them and escorted them out to the sheriff's car."

"Leroy was blubbering like a baby when he came to. I knew from the start there was something about that boy I didn't like." Nana frowned.

I would've rolled my eyes if they didn't hurt so much. "You and I both, right Nana?"

She nodded in acknowledgment as she gave my hand a big squeeze.

"Oh, honey. I thought you were dead. Well, maybe not dead, but I was so concerned." Big tears dripped from Nana's watery blue eyes. "But, we're in for another long haul."

"It's all right, Nana. We're safe." I blinked back tears that wanted to flow.

Dee Dee balled her fists and dragged a chair up to sit eye to eye with me. Voice low, she laid out the skinny. "Joyce was screaming circumstantial evidence, and that she knows a heck of a good lawyer. Sheriff will have to go back to the drawing board to prove our story in court."

"I have a big surprise for Joyce and Leroy. Where are my clothes? Is my sweater here?" I surveyed the room. If Dee Dee had taken any longer to answer I would've panicked.

"Sure, they're in the closet." Dee Dee pointed to the white door. "But you're not going anywhere, yet. I'm your private guard until the doctor says you can go." She looked like she was taking this guard position very seriously.

"I don't want to wear my sweater. Get it and I'll show you."

Someone hesitantly knocked on the door. It opened just enough for a head to poke through.

"Is it all right if I come in?"

"Sure, Sheriff, come on in." I held my head as high as I could and grasped my sweater from Dee Dee. "You're just in time."

CHAPTER THIRTY

How are you feeling? You gave everyone quite a scare." I swear Sheriff Wheeler winked at Nana.

"I think I'll live. Thanks for asking." Did I just thank the enemy? Maybe it was the result of being under the influence of pain meds. Or maybe it was the image of a handsome man in a crisp, form fitting uniform.

I held my breath as I reached into my sweater pocket. Yes! There it was—the tape recorder. I took it out and presented it to Sheriff Wheeler.

"Sheriff, I hope this will help in the case against Joyce and Leroy. I think I got her full confession on tape. It should be enough to put them away for a long time."

He stared at the recorder as if it were made of gold.

"How about it Sheriff, can we listen to it?"

He nodded and I handed the small unit to my best friend. "Dee Dee, you want to do the honors?"

After all, it was her freedom at stake, plus I was just too dang tired.

She took it from me and switched it on. Silence veiled the room as we listened to Joyce tell her tale of woe. Yes, the Haygoods had been done wrong, but as the saying goes, "Two wrongs don't make a right."

Sheriff Wheeler left a happy man. He assured us that with the evidence they had, and now the taped confession, he had enough for the DA. Not only had the murder of John Tatum been solved, but the long ago murder of Donnie Haygood could be put to rest.

I thought nothing could shock me after all that had happened that weekend. I was wrong. The sheriff had one more trick up his sleeve. After thanking me profusely for my help, he walked over and kissed me gently on the forehead. "You did good, Trixie."

Before I had time to respond, he turned on his heels and made his escape.

Nana and Dee Dee snickered like teenage girls. Since I couldn't throw anything, I took a play out of Nana's book and stuck my tongue out at them.

My how I love those two girls!

It was hard to believe a month had passed since that terrible time in Dahlonega.

Remnants of Thanksgiving dinner, turkey and dressing, mashed potatoes with gravy, green beans and all the trimmings, garnered Mama's table. Mama and Nana were cleaning up the kitchen. I sat on the couch, my leg propped up on pillows. The fall I took on my knee had forced me to undergo surgery at long last. The doctor cleaned it out and repaired what he could. A total knee replacement was delayed, he told me, but not for long.

I heard Beau's laughter from the kitchen, and my heart rate kicked up a notch. Since returning home, Mama's handsome neighbor and I had tiptoed into a budding relationship.

"You want some pumpkin pie?" Beau brushed his hand across my chin, and kissed me lightly on the lips.

It felt so good to be home among family and friends. The heat from the fire warmed me on the outside while my family and friends warmed me on the inside.

Beau tucked an afghan over my legs. "Sure you don't need anything?"

"All I need is right here." I gave him an appreciative look, a blush rising from his attention—but just under the flush of newfound affection, there lingered that dull ache of loss.

"Well don't you two look snuggly?" Nana came in carrying a tray of mugs filled with hot chocolate. She didn't miss a thing.

"Nana, don't get jealous. You know you're still my best girlfriend," Beau shot back. He went over to Nana, bent down, and gave her a kiss on her cheek.

She turned red as a beet, and playfully slapped him on his arm, "Oh, Beau, get outta here."

My heart melted a little watching him treat Nana with such kindness and caring. Maybe, just maybe, this heart of mine would mend under Beau's attention.

"You know? I could use a boyfriend, too. You think that Sheriff in Dahlonega might want to take me to the movies?" I couldn't believe my ears. Dee Dee hadn't mentioned the idea of a boyfriend since had Gary died.

For better or for worse, the incident in Dahlonega had changed all of us.

Dee Dee and I had gone over the events more than once. Our near death experience had deepened our friendship, and neither of us looked at life the same way.

Joyce and Leroy had decided to take matters into their own hands when life hadn't gone their way. And for what? Not only were they unable to save their beloved inn, but irony had kicked them in the bum.

I'd just recently received a note from Sueleigh with good news. John Tatum had come through for their daughter after all. Unbeknownst to everyone except his lawyer, he'd changed his will to read that if something should happen to him, she would inherit a large portion of his wealth, including the inn. Joyce and Leroy handed it to her on a silver platter.

Sueleigh's daughter finally received what she deserved. Not the inn, but recognition from her father. Sueleigh expressed her undying love and told us that if we ever needed a place to stay while visiting Dahlonega, it was on the house. As for me, I didn't plan on going back anytime soon.

Frank Dalton, Sueleigh's father, was exonerated on murder charges, but had to stand trial for blackmail. Donnie Haygood's murderer had long since been dead. But at least Donnie could rest in peace knowing the truth was out in the open.

I wrote the story of a lifetime for Harv. Two murders solved made for a happy editor, but I told him not to expect every story to be so exciting. I was in Harv's good graces and I had passed my six-month probation period. Life was good!

Thank you, Father.

QUESTIONS FOR DISCUSSION

- There was a period of time, after Trixie's difficult divorce, when she struggled with her faith. Have you ever experienced a time in your life similar to Trixie's. If so, what are some ways you overcame those feelings?

- When Trixie moved home she rekindled a friendship with her long-time friend Dee Dee. She encouraged Trixie to let go of past hurts and move towards a faith-filled future. Do you think it's important to have friends who will encourage your faith? If so, why?

- When Trixie first met Sueleigh Dalton, she judged her on her appearance. She then realized there was much more to Sueleigh than how she looked. Have you, or someone you know, been judged on how you look? Can we miss out on knowing a person for who they really are if we judge on appearance only?

- Joyce and Leroy took matters into their own hands when life didn't go their way. They felt justified in taking the life of another person. Can you think of a time in the Bible when someone did wrong, but felt justified in doing so?

- Nana is a little spit-fire. She is not going to sit in a rocking chair just because she has a little age on her. Do you know a Nana or have a Nana in your life?

- What was your favorite scene? Why?

- Who was your favorite character? Why?

CPSIA information can be obtained at www.ICGtesting.com
Printed in the USA
LVOW071257161111

255249LV00001B/200/P